BUFFALO NOIR

EDITED BY ED PARK & BRIGID HUGHES

This collection is comprised of works of fiction. All names, characters, places, and incidents are the product of the authors' imaginations. Any resemblance to real events or persons, living or dead, is entirely coincidental.

Published by Akashic Books
©2015 Akashic Books

Series concept by Tim McLoughlin and Johnny Temple
Buffalo map by Aaron Petrovich

ISBN: 978-1-61775-381-7
Library of Congress Control Number: 2015934036

First printing

Printed in Canada

Akashic Books
Twitter: @AkashicBooks
Facebook: AkashicBooks
E-mail: info@akashicbooks.com
Website: www.akashicbooks.com

MIX
Paper from
responsible source
FSC® C00407

ALSO IN THE AKASHIC NOIR SERIES

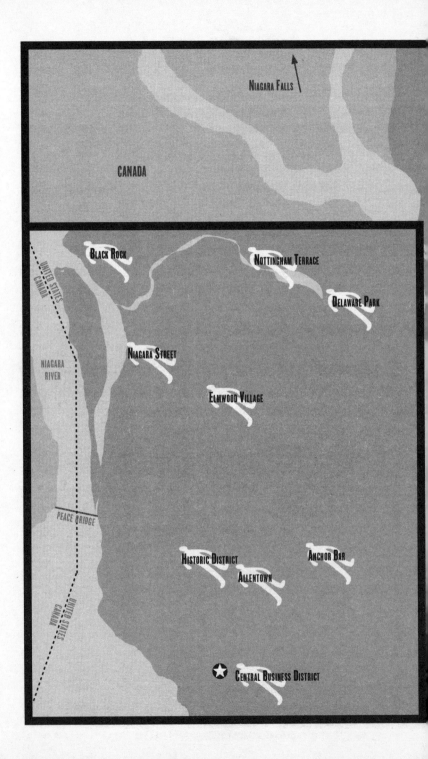

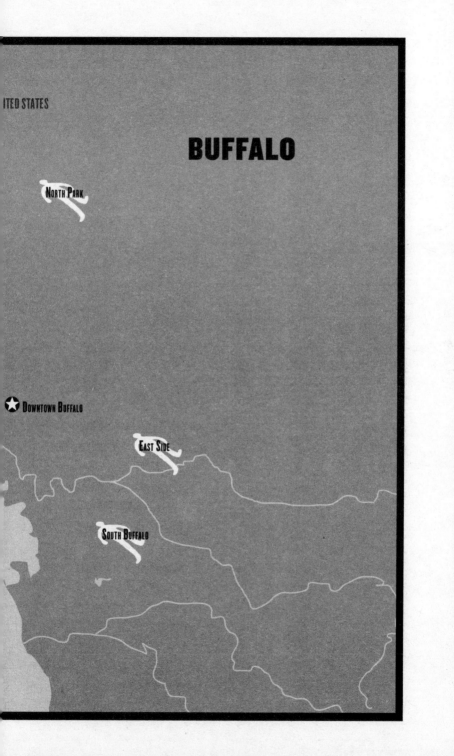

TABLE OF CONTENTS

PART III: BLOODLINES

INTRODUCTION
Ice-Cold Stories

To this day I don't know if it was a dream. I was a high school student in Buffalo, New York, when Van Halen's 1986 album *5150* was released. A radio station called my house around seven in the evening, when I was groggy from a postdinner nap. They were calling because my parents' phone number ended in 5150. It made perfect sense. I don't recall what I said, only that the deejay seemed disappointed by my confused replies. When asked what my favorite radio station was, I answered honestly, mentioning the call letters of a competitor. After I hung up I had this feeling I'd been broadcast live on the air. I didn't mention it to anyone at home, nor at school the next day. Maybe no one had heard me. Maybe it was all in my head.

Van Halen entitled their album *5150* after the California penal code tag for "criminally insane." Curiously, my father was (and is) a psychiatrist. Though he did not specialize in forensics, by the time of the call (which, now, reads more dreamlike to me), he had already served as a psychiatric examiner for Buffalo's most notorious criminal trial of the 1980s: the case of the .22 killer.

At nine thirty p.m. on September 22, 1980, Robert Oddo, seventeen, walks into the Tops supermarket on Genesee Street in Buffalo. He notices a "white male with a hooded sweatshirt" sitting outside, a shopping bag near his feet. A half hour later, a fourteen-year-old is shot three times in the head while waiting in a car for a friend. Oddo spots the man with the bag, fleeing on foot. The "dopey"-looking shooter has "wavy, light-brown hair" and "silver metal glasses." The victim is black.

The shopping bag was used to catch the shell casings.

Over the next few days, three more African American men are killed in separate incidents, the first two in the Buffalo area and the last one in nearby Niagara Falls. A witness to the first murder, in the parking lot of a Cheektowaga Burger King, says she saw a man in his twenties, dressed in khaki, holding a crumpled grocery bag.

Recovered shell casings and bullet fragments indicate the same .22-caliber weapon. Witnesses describe the shooter as white.

The October 6 entry on the time line published in the *Courier-Express* notes that the chief of homicide "meets for five hours with an astrologist and a psychic in hopes they will lead him to the .22-caliber killer."

A few days later, "the bodies of two black Buffalo-area cab drivers, their hearts cut out, are found." Authorities believe the crimes are related to the earlier killings.

Through the rest of the year, there are mysterious stabbings of dark-skinned men in New York and again in Buffalo, also believed to be linked.

Fear and frustration grip the city. Demonstrations in front of city hall. Awards for any tips leading to arrest.

No answers.

A phantom killer, exacerbating racial tension.

In January of 1981, down in Fort Benning, Georgia, a white army private attempts to stab a black soldier. He's thrown in the stockade.

His name is Joseph Christopher, and he is from Buffalo.

Noir, of course, is French for *black*. We've used it for over half a century to indicate atmosphere, a mix of mystery and grit, even a certain glamour applied to a tale of crime and violence. But is the term itself racist? One esteemed African American writer I contacted for this book, a writer I'd hoped would contribute, played naive when I asked if he would contribute. He wrote back, *What do you mean by noir?* Our discussion ended. But he made his point.

In this story, noir means noir. But it also means black. And for me—someone whose parents came to Buffalo from Seoul, Korea, in the late sixties—I'm interested in all the shades in between white and black.

Joseph Christopher is brought back to his hometown. After over half a year spent in the Erie County Holding Center, he waives the right to a lawyer, determined to represent himself. The photo in the *Buffalo News* shows a baby-faced young man in a dark jacket, delta of white at the neck. Ghost of a smile. His wavy hair is parted away from his forehead, and he has what appears to be a light mustache and nascent goatee. He looks like a mellow hippie. He looks like Tiny Tim. Then you see that the belt at the bottom of the frame is actually the chain binding his wrists close in front of him.

1981 goes by. One day my father and I are at a mall—Boulevard or Eastern Hills. The wide corridors are the closest thing to a public square. In those days there was a small TV screen embedded in a sort of stalk or column rising from the ground. Usually no one pays much attention, but on this afternoon, people are swarming around the stalk. We wedge in for a better view. Tumult on the screen. President Reagan has been shot.

Later, Joseph Christopher waives a jury trial, wanting the judge to decide his fate. One-on-one. My father is brought in as one of several psychiatric examiners to determine whether he is competent to stand trial. His assessment is that Christopher needs psychiatric treatment before this is possible.

From the *Courier-Express*:

> *Dr. Park said when he first saw Christopher in the Erie County Holding Center the defendant was lying on his cot in a cell with a white towel draped over his face. The witness said he was told Christopher spends much of his time this way.*
>
> *Asked the significance of the towel over Christopher's head, Dr. Park replied: "It has something to do with his wish to ward off external stimuli and concentrate more on his own thinking."*
>
> *The defense lawyer asked Dr. Park his thoughts on Christopher's continuous smile, even at inappropriate times during psychiatric interviews.*
>
> *"It is my opinion he was sensing triumph over the situation," the witness responded, "knowing he has control over examinations by psychiatrists. He feels triumphant when he feels other people don't understand him."*

Tom Toles, the *Buffalo News* cartoonist who would later win the Pulitzer Prize, drew a judge regarding a swarm of bickering psychiatrists with distaste. The caption read, *If you ask me, you're the crazy ones!*

Be that as it may, I find the whole episode unsettling. Decades later, it continues to fascinate me. At the time my father was the director of the psychiatric consultation service at the Erie County Medical Center. Even then I could tell it consumed him. He thought about it all the time. On the evening news they showed a courtroom sketch of him testifying.

* * *

Christopher's relationship with his father is fraught. Effeminate, soft-faced, he can't seem to please his macho dad. Devastated after his father's passing, Christopher mans up and joins the army, as if to prove himself.

That's one way of looking at it. Who knows the truth?

Maybe his wish for the judge to determine his fate, rather than a jury, is a wish for approval. *Who's not man enough now? I joined the army. I've killed people.*

From the *Courier-Express*:

> *The psychiatrist . . . testified that the defendant's personality underwent a "marked change" after the recent death of his father.*
>
> *Christopher became "very despondent," said Dr. Park, visited his father's grave almost daily, felt he wished to die himself, and began diassociating himself from close friends . . .*

"Psychiatrist Says Paranoia Keeps Christopher Mum"
—headline, *Buffalo News*

Some interjections by Joseph Christopher:

"Is it peculiar to part your hair on one side or the other without giving a reason?"

"If I had sat in my cell and looked at the wall and said nothing, what analogy would you have made?"

"I don't believe I refused to say why I didn't eat in Georgia."

"I'm not normal?"

At the time of the trial, my father was forty-five, exactly the age I am now. *Isn't it something,* he wrote to me recently, when I asked him about the case, *that we sometimes remember things vividly for such a long time?*

When I was ten, who did I think I would be at forty-five?
This introduction is a time machine.

I associate the trial with Buffalo, with my childhood there. (I
was ten.) After a long time, anything can seem like a dream.
This one, I suppose, is a nightmare—it haunted me growing
up. Fascinated me. My own private Buffalo noir. Did someone
really call me that night in 1986? Was there really a courtroom
sketch of my dad? At least I know the Toles cartoon is real—a
copy of it hangs in my father's study. In a cabinet, unseen for
years, he kept a mound of clippings from the *Buffalo News* and
the *Courier-Express*. The latter paper shuttered in 1982. We got
the *News*, so my father must have been collecting the other
paper the day it appeared.

Looking at them now, I'm as interested by the texture of the
paper, the extraneous information, as with the case itself. A mention of Jack Kemp. An ad for Sibley's. The winning lottery number for April 11, 1982, for crying out loud. (It was 168.)

My past is here. My past in Buffalo.

The yellowing newspapers, the fading black-and-white, is
noir.

Years in the making, *Buffalo Noir* is finally ready. My coeditor
Brigid Hughes and I reached out to people we knew and people
we didn't, expats and lifelong Buffalonians and current residents
who came from somewhere else. People recommended other
people. I'm knocked out by the range of modes and moods, the
different neighborhoods portrayed and eras evoked. The tal-
ent on display here could power the First Niagara Center for a
Stanley Cup run. (We can always hope, right?)

The book kicks off with Christina Milletti's exploration of
madness, set partly in that most noir-cum-Gothic structure, the
Buffalo Psychiatric Center, its looming towers designed by H.H.
Richardson in 1870. And then we go everywhere. John Wray and

Brooke Costello offer up a wonderfully woolly anecdote featuring a cameo by one of the great weird products of the Queen City, Rick James. The legendary Joyce Carol Oates, who has fictionalized the area many times in her long and brilliant career, gives us Buffalo-as-Buffalo in an intense, squalled-out story. Lissa Marie Redmond, a for-real Buffalo detective, working the cold-case department, gives us an ice-cold story of lake-effect chills. Gary Earl Ross's "Good Neighbors" unfolds with a dreadful, fablelike inevitability, there in the heart of Allentown—where its characters might encounter the enigmatic figure in the story by Dimitri Anastasopoulos.

Connie Porter, author of *All-Bright Court*, returns home with "Peace Bridge," and S.J. Rozan recreates the city that she lived in when she studied architecture in Buffalo. Tom Fontana gives us the best kind of barstool rambling that's all diverting enough—until things go south. Buffalo State professor Kim Chinquee, whose perfect short short stories I've been tracking in the journal *NOON* for years, closes things out with the haunting "Hand."

And it gives me particular satisfaction that Lawrence Block, whose creations include the hard-boiled detective Matt Scudder and gentleman thief Bernie Rhodenbarr, here definitively makes his native city the setting for the escapades of one of his most diabolically entertaining creations: Ehrengraf, the well-dressed lawyer who never loses a case. (Better think twice about hiring him—you'll know him from his impeccable necktie knot.)

This book is full of shadows and secrets—and everywhere around it seems to fall the snow that Buffalonians aren't just used to but are defined by: beautiful, elemental, sometimes deadly.

On December 17, 1981, the *Courier-Express* runs the headline: "Christopher Ruled Unfit to Stand Trial."

In the corner of A-1, the weather: "WINTRY. Flurries. Some snow this afternoon, tonight. High upper 20s, low teens."

Ed Park
August 2015

PART I

Buffalo Unveiled

DR. KIRKBRIDE'S MORAL TREATMENT PLAN

BY Christina Milletti

Elmwood Village

I f irony had a flavor, it would taste like steel. Oxidized. Unforgiving. My tongue is rusty from it when I phone my son on Saturday mornings. We get ten minutes. He won't give me five.

"Are you through, Mom?" he says when I tell him I love him. He hangs up. Every week it's the same thing.

A large metal door separates me from my children. Plexiglass. Fiber-optic cables. From the outside, the walls of the Richardson Complex look worn, the stone etched by snow and time. But the interior is scarred by a far worse erosion. The patients here roam halls eaten away by generations of rats. Joists rotting from seasonal ice dams. Our minds are as creaky as Ward E's floors. When I wake in the morning, plaster has rained down from the ceiling; a fine sand coats my sheets. Perhaps I'm just molting, my skin flaking away so that, one day, I can be someone else. Someone new.

Before I was sent here, there were rumors the mayor planned to shut the asylum's doors. Eject the so-called "moderate" cases outside the gates. Let the obdurate winds drive unwanted inmates downtown. To the empty warehouses and silos. Maybe into Lake Erie itself. The plan, I heard, was to reclaim the complex. Restore the bones of the building. Transform it. Maybe into a posh hotel.

Keep the form, but not the crazy content.

I don't blame the mayor. It's easy to picture chandeliers in our grand foyer. The fourth-floor chapel made up as a ballroom. Even the signature towers—helmeted sentries above the patients inside—refitted as suites for political sponsors. Like all things in Buffalo, the plan had stalled. But it would get moving again. In six months. A year.

With better timing, a "moderate" case like me would have been left to myself. Tricked out with an anklet. At home.

My luck never changes.

From my therapist: *What do you make of that?*

Once again, the taste of rust swells, coats my tongue.

I close my eyes so she can't see me rolling them.

I thought that I'd left my problems behind, that I'd buried them in the many yards of the many places I've called home since I met my husband. The dorm Ed and I filled with books, a futon, a used recliner. Later, a rented house with sloping floors. Then, when Ed joined Hampton, Payne, and Lynch, LLC, a tony, compact apartment seated off an upscale cul-de-sac not far from the Albright-Knox Art Gallery. We used to walk its mossy paths while Bobby, just a colicky infant then, howled shamelessly from his squeaky pram, much to the art lovers' dismay.

They glared. Ed laughed. His audacity once amused me.

Our last home was the farmhouse. Our Clarence farmhouse.

Now, we will never move into the home I imagined. The home Ed promised. The one thing I've always wanted. The one thing, it seems, I can never have.

If the past is the lens through which you observe the present, the one lesson I've learned—perhaps the only lesson I've ever learned—is that it's impossible to change your perspective. Only your eyesight changes. Which is to say: over time it gets worse.

Tell me your story, Dr. Kirkbride now counsels. *Not his. Yours.*

The sun streams in lavishly through the barred windows. We should all feel its heat the same way.

"My story, doctor?"

Call me Cheryl, she says.

Her linen skirt whispers against the Naugahyde chair, and I suddenly perceive a new sense to my words. Cheryl doesn't hear it. But then Ed often plants thoughts in my mind.

"Mystery, doctor?"

She makes a mark in her notepad.

"There's nothing mysterious about it," I say.

Meaning?

I just look at her. She knows precisely what I mean.

Write it all down, Jane, she says, handing me paper and pencil.

A sign of trust.

So I do.

The past has a bit more give than we like to acknowledge. Like a fat man on a bus you squeeze by to get a free seat, it can make you wonder if the crush was worth the trouble. But if you exert your will, the past teeters a bit, makes an opening for you where before there was none. As for that unwelcome residue that gums up your clothing? Well, you might say it's the gooey evidence of what, in better times, I called desire. Now I simply reach for the hand sanitizer, and chalk up my chapped, antiseptic hands to the unpredictable pitch and heave of "desire's" obnoxious cousin: "change."

Bluster?

Cheryl has scrawled the word in the corner of my latest draft.

That's one word for it. When there's no other option, what else do you have?

Cheryl would no doubt say "the truth."

The truth is that it's been almost a year since the rest of the world noticed Ed disappeared. What they don't know is that he took off long before that.

But no one believes me.

Why would anyone believe a wife who claims that, one day, her husband went to work on his book in his study. And he, quite simply, never came out?

Dr. Kirkbride once had the audacity to ask whether I was "aware" that getting "lost in a book," as she put it, is "just an expression."

To some questions there are no answers.

I've told her: I did not kill Ed. I have no idea where he is. I've told the police the same thing. I've explained to anyone who would listen: I have no idea what Ed was writing. Nor why. I've even admitted that every time I write my husband's name now— every time I try to account for our life and his disappearance— Ed seems to be standing behind me. Looking over my shoulder. His hot breath raising the hairs of my neck.

Right now I feel him. He wants me to stop.

Ed has never left me at all.

The day my husband disappeared began much like any other. It was a school day. Ed was already hard at work on his book— he'd taken to sleeping on the couch in his study in order to, as he put it, "expedite his memory." So it was left to me to wake up our son, push him into the bathroom, then persuade Bobby to brush his teeth, wash his face, and wrestle his cowlick in place—all the while bracing the baby with my tender left tennis elbow. Then, down to the kitchen the three of us went for breakfast, only twenty minutes to spare before the school bus was due to take Bobby to Harris Hill Elementary. With the exception of Ed's growing remoteness (which at that time struck me as not so very different from the absences of other fathers who left for work before their children woke), our family that morning could have been any other in our neighborhood. The sun streamed in the windows. The smell of lawn pesticides lingered above the dew in the air. The baby drooled on a toy in her playpen. It was peaceful. It was boring. I'm sure I felt restless.

Now I miss those days the way an amputee misses a limb.

As usual, Bobby was running late, his book bag was only half packed, and he was wearing two different socks. But he was in a good mood. Ed roared at him from behind his office door as Bobby rocketed down the hallway.

Naturally, my son found it amusing.

"He's p.o.'d," Bobby grinned as he climbed into his chair.

It was one of Ed's pet phrases, one of those I'd always disliked. It made Ed sound peevish, like an old lady fussing over a pile of dog crap steaming on her front lawn. Maybe that's why when Bobby said it he made me smile—a boy channeling a father who was (in turn) impersonating a crabby octogenarian. In Bobby's squeaky adolescent pitch, I could hear Ed's voice. But because it was Bobby, not Ed, I'd laugh.

I put my hand over my smile (I didn't want to encourage him), as Bobby went to explain that his friend/nemesis Jimmy (it was hard to keep track) had been making trouble for him on the bus. But as syrup dripped from his chin, and he smacked his lips contentedly, I set my fears aside. There was nothing to worry about. He was high-strung and, like a monkey, tight and lean. Bobby could fend for himself, even if his heart was as impressionable as clay.

"Talk to your father," I advised, then flipped a pancake. A moment later, I slid it onto his plate.

Naturally, I knew Ed wouldn't answer a knock on his door. He'd stopped answering knocks a month before. Recently, he rarely showed up for dinner. I should have been more concerned. But, at the time, his absence was a relief.

I no longer had to negotiate his moods.

Bobby could have used Ed's help. My son was long-limbed and fast, but Jimmy Hammond—a bloated-face boy whose sweat smelled like onions—was fond of roughing kids up. Bully was in his future, everyone knew it. Everyone, that is, but his mother, Regina. A birdlike woman who held her shoulders like wings, she chirped at parties about her son's wit, while Jimmy's wiry, absentminded father looked on in disbelief. How Regina gave

birth to a brute like Jimmy is one of the mysteries of genetics
. . . unless you believed a popular neighborhood rumor that
Jimmy's egg rolled from an illegitimate nest. The current can-
didate was a strapping pool boy who stopped by Regina's home
every Thursday while her husband was off at work.

Back then, I defended her. How young I once was.

"It's nice to see an independent woman get what she wants,"
I said, backing myself against Ed's crotch, knocking him off balance. He laughed, cuffed me away.

"Maybe later," he said.

As usual, later never came.

Now I wonder: was that the instant Regina appeared on his
radar? Would this story have been completely different if I'd just
kept my thoughts, my soft-boiled ass, to myself?

Of course, I wouldn't have had to look so hard for the pi-
ranha hiding within the school of sharks if Ed hadn't moved us
north of the city to Clarence, to a so-called gateway development zone—an experimental neighborhood built by one of his
clients, wedged between the muscular outer suburbs and the
svelte inner exurbs, designed to appeal (so the pamphlet read)
to "young, upwardly mobile homeowners looking for outer space
and inner peace, for self-discovery and future fortune. Mean age:
38. No. of children: 1. No. of cars. 2. No. of homes: 1.5."

Ed's client had built the community on the homestead of
an old barley estate. The original farmhouse itself was in good
condition, and it stood as the heart of the neighborhood's newly
built vistas where the development brochure still pictures (I'm
told) a "community center anchored by an organic garden, kite
shop, gallery space, and day spa." Ed whistled when he showed
it to me. The new homes were a marvel, tricked out with solar
panels, geothermal floors, whirlpools, saunas, and media rooms.
"We'll be at the center of all that," he said. "Not bad for a barley
farm, right?"

True, the farmhouse was a steal. Sure, Ed was doing his

CHRISTINA MILLETTI // 27

wealthy client a favor. All that fresh air, meanwhile, was terrific for Bobby. But couldn't we have foreseen the effect our new-old home would have on us? Shouldn't we have known that moving into a farmhouse—no matter how quaintly maintained or historically fetching—surrounded by a dozen newly pointed mini-mansions was simply a bad idea? That our neighbors, high on the chemical outgas of new-home aroma, would begin to resent the mortality that our farmhouse—cast right in their sight line—stood for? All too soon, we'd feel under siege, all those eyes on us, just waiting for the house to be razed.

It was all supposed to be temporary. "Just one year," Ed assured me. After that, his client was going to pay us a reasonable markup to move out, knock the farmhouse over, and build the spa in its place. The plans were on course. And then the Clarence Historical Society got wind of the scheme. Suddenly, the farmhouse was the county's "last emblem of pre-Fordian Agriculture and Animal Matrimonial Heritage." A legal intervention was filed and we weren't stuck, so much as waylaid, in a lawsuit against both Ed's client and Erie County. One year became three. Then Ed started writing. Quit his job. And once our credit tanked, well, then we were stranded. So when Ed's tune about the farmhouse changed, I wasn't surprised. His new pitch was persuasive. "We're the cheapest house in an upscale neighborhood," he argued. "Moving?" He waved his hands about. "Why would we want to do that? When we sell we'll make a killing. Move farther out. To the exurbs proper." We'd be set, he went on. Two middle-class kids would finally make good.

We wouldn't just nail the American dream to our doormat, he explained. We'd wipe our muddy shoes on it too.

"We'll show them," he said, pointing outside vaguely. At the time, I thought he meant our neighbors. The Historical Society staff. His former client. My mother.

Ed said it more firmly the second time: "We'll show them what's *what*."

I must have sighed, because he wrapped me up his arms. "Come on, Janey." He was so warm then. "Let's just see it through."

Ed wasn't just a lawyer. He was a salesman. All good lawyers are.

So I held my tongue. Dressed up our old girl of a home the way a retiree distracts from her sagging chin by plastering her cheeks with rouge. But our neighbors' front lawns were our front lines, and all that staring wore me down. Predawn joggers and postbreakfast strollers. Loose children and lost dogs. Midnight insomniacs and early risers. It wasn't the looking itself that troubled me. Even I look in other people's windows. Sometimes intentionally. But our family had made a subtle move from curiosity to *entertainment*. We were "them." The hothouse drama at center stage. We didn't belong. And it became more than evident as our neighbors sat on their porches sipping cocktails and nibbling overpriced cheese that they excused their bad behavior because they believed we were conditional. "Visitors" at best. "Interlopers" at worst. We'd be gone soon, they thought. So they lurked and peeped, scrutinized our dull program of getting to work, reprimanding our children, washing dishes, paying bills. How humdrum. Still they watched. Their hot eyes fixed on the backs of our necks.

Of all our neighbors, Regina Hammond seemed the most sincere. Which is to say, she craved sincerity the way a goldfish craves ocean—an idea out of her depth. I try to be kind to myself: How could I have known that she had her eye on Ed from the start? That she'd suck off my husband while I nursed in the next room? That by the time I'd fixed my shirt, he'd fixed his fly.

The moral of the story is simple: the nicest neighbor behind your fence is malevolent once they walk through your gate.

Don't let their feet crush your grass. Stir up the brush.

Duck your head. Turn the hasp.

Don't let them see your fear.

* * *

On the day Ed disappeared, I was focused exclusively on getting Bobby to the bus on time with a hot meal in his stomach. My movements were economical from long experience. I signed a test, flipped a pancake, made myself a cup of coffee without moving more than two feet in any direction. I even spared a moment to coo to the baby who, sitting hunched like a frog in her playpen, was happily beating a wood spoon on the rail, making the kind of insistent, percussive music only infant ears can love.

For a mother, I was at peak performance.

How little I once knew.

Bobby kept talking. I washed the dishes. The cat, meanwhile, had curled up at my feet. I had hold of a plate, a pan, a carton of milk. I barely listened as Bobby rambled on about his homework—something about polar bears and mortality rates—when I began to wash the boning knife. Why it was out, I'll never know. At the time, I'm sure I simply thought Ed had taken it out of the drawer by mistake. He knew as much about boning knives as he did about salad forks: it was all the same to him.

My husband remains a peasant at heart. I always liked that about him.

I soaped the knife. There was a small stain on the handle that would not come off. As anyone might, I soaped it, rinsed it again. Raising the knife high in the sunlight, I turned it around to get a better look. The light glinted. I saw my face in the blade.

Then the knife wasn't in my hands. And Bobby's cat began to hiss.

What happened at that moment isn't so much a blur as a series of disconnected snapshots that remain bound together in my memory by virtue of my own disbelief. How, after all, could the knife have slipped from my hand with such force? Such fortuitous aim? Yet this one hadn't just slid from my hand, but shot across the room and lodged itself in my son's left thigh. We stared at each other. Bobby was so surprised, he didn't cry out. Mouth agape, he simply stared at me, a wad of half-chewed pancake crammed in his left cheek, as the wound went white before the blood rushed back, welled up, began to drip between us on the floor. It was quiet. The cat stared. The baby watched. Outside, the landscapers put aside their edgers. Even the procession of morning traffic suddenly ceased its inevitable parade by our home. It wasn't until I heard Ed's Royal typewriter ring upstairs, in fact, that we began to move again, slowly, trying to assume the roles we'd once portrayed like the costumes I suddenly perceived they were. That's what I learned that day: a husband can become a monster; a son, a victim; a mother, a killer—in just an instant. That's all it takes for a new label to stick.

We are never quite who we think we are.

"Mom?" Bobby said. He was looking down at the knife hilt-deep in his skin, his leg like a ham hock being prepped for dinner. The knife wobbled tenderly as he panted tiny iridescent gasps. Then with a yank—I tried to stop him—he pulled the blade from his thigh.

Bobby has always been decisive. Just like his father.

"Stop!"

How long did it take me to move? Ten seconds? Twelve? Too long to rush to his side—to comfort him—to grab a batter-slick towel and bind his leg in a poor tourniquet that did little to abate the flow.

"Ed!" I'm sure I screamed. "For Christ's sake, Ed!"

There was no answer, and I had no time to coddle my reclusive husband from the half-light of his lair.

"Let's go," I said. Bobby stared at me blankly. "Your dad will meet us at the hospital."

What else did I say? I can't recall. I know I kept a steady rap going to keep us focused as I moved him from the chair toward the car, then ran back for the baby. "Take my hand," I'm sure I told him as I pulled him upright. "That's good. Your arm on my

CHRISTINA MILLETTI // 31

waist. Now, all your weight on me." Finally we were hobbling toward the door. "That's just fine. You're doing great. Look how brave you are."

He was observing me with a singleness of attention that I hadn't felt since he was a tiny wrinkled pup curled in the crook of my arm.

"Mom?"

We were joined at the hip as we made our way to the car, but we were now also connected in a more profound fashion, as though the knife that had broken his skin had also penetrated other less permeable barriers—the ones between thoughts, between mother and son, between a child and himself.

"Mom," he was asking, "what happened there? Why did you hurt me, Mom? Did I do something wrong? Mom, why isn't Dad coming with us?"

In her car seat behind him, the baby burped, oblivious to the wreckage of her brother's leg or the pain in my lungs. I could not breathe. I could not answer even one of Bobby's questions.

After that, we never saw Ed again.

Before me, Dr. Kirkbride is rapt. Her hair is blond and looks as crisp as a dried copse of cuttleweed. The urge to touch it is hard to resist.

It's not unusual for survivors of emotional violence to develop obstructive, often dangerous behaviors that inhibit, or preclude, emotional and physical intimacy, she says, her voice neutral, as she tilts her head. *Such patterns tend to get worse with age.* She pauses. *Were they a nuisance to your marriage?*

She asks the question so politely, I'm nearly disarmed. I fail to realize, for a moment, that she's referring to me, not Ed. But I pinch myself—hard—no doubt adding another bruise to my thighs.

"We had some troubles."

It's the nature of her occupation that mildly gloomy disclosures make her happy. A soothing, birdlike sound warbles in the back of her throat. Then, just as I think it's time to go—as I begin to gather my paper-thin housecoat and rise from my chair—she shoots off a final question, as though it's suddenly occurred to her.

Was Ed a good father?

She's smiling. She knows she's caught me off guard. Just as she intended.

"Of course. Ed loved his children."

My tone isn't defensive. But my qualifier undermines all my hard work. Every "I'm sure," "no doubt," and "of course," she's told me, augments uncertainty rather than diminishing it. The more convinced I seem, in short, the more skeptical she becomes. And she doesn't hide it.

On her wall, beneath her diplomas, Cheryl has hung a print of the Richardson Complex when it first opened: when its sandstone walls were surrounded by endless lawns and gardens and its tall windows weren't covered with grime.

When all the patients were bathed in light.

"What did they call your work back then?" I ask. "A moral treatment plan?"

Cheryl can't help looking pleased.

You know about my grandfather?

I shrug. During our mandated "library encounter time," I had skimmed a book about the building's design, and the first Dr. Kirkbride's—her grandfather's—revolutionary patient care "strategy."

"Do you think it works?"

She considers my question carefully. *Do you?*

I sigh. She is single-minded. "I did not kill Ed."

We stare at each other, like parents fighting when their children aren't far enough out of earshot. Dr. Kirkbride can project an uncanny silence when she chooses. I can't even hear her breathe.

As for me, the stress makes my eczema flare—my elbows start to itch, then the back of my neck. Even the inflamed patch on my left hip.

She watches me squirm. A look, like sadness, in her eyes. There's no getting through to her.

Then our time is up, the session breaks. Out in the hall once again, an orderly at my side, I give in. By the time we negotiate our way down the curved hallway back to the female ward, my fingernails are wet with shredded skin and blood.

The orderly doesn't say a word. He just hands me a bandage. Then he's gone down the hall, the rubber soles of his orthopedic shoes squeaking softly on the old tiles. The sound is intolerable. It is comforting.

I am torn in so many ways.

Occasionally Regina calls on me. She waits in the visitors' center, legs neatly crossed at her ankles.

A year hasn't changed her. Two years haven't changed her.

I want to reach out and slap her face.

Dr. Kirkbride has encouraged these meetings. She's advised me to meet with my former neighbor, to *reconcile* (as she puts it) *your memories. If not your stories.*

Regina is the person who called the police when Ed went missing, two weeks after Bobby's trip to the ER. Evidently, she expected Ed to check in each night. Me? I expected him to be writing his book.

"Regina," I said, as I opened the farmhouse door that day. Then, as the officers strolled up behind her: "You've brought friends."

Of course they weren't my friends. Regina wasn't my friend. Yet they allowed her to take Bobby to play in her yard while they asked me their questions. Regina has no shame.

"Someone has to look for Ed," she said as she turned to go. "You should have called the police days ago." She looked around, took in the curtains drawn over the windows. Then she was gone. And I was left with two officers in their sturdy square shoes weighing down my farmhouse floor.

"She's fucking my husband," I said, when they asked where Ed was, why he hadn't been heard from for days. When they said nothing, didn't register even a hint of surprise, I foolishly offered the truth.

"He's disappeared," I told them. "One day Ed was here, the next day he wasn't." I've repeated the same story ever since.

The officers asked other questions. Bobby's injury came up. I did my best to explain how the knife slipped. They nodded, took notes, then politely asked to look in Ed's office.

The light was shining in the east window as I opened the door to his study. Ed's typewriter sat idle on his desk, papers stacked in a neat pile beside it. A lone sharpened pencil lay on the blotter. His chair was tucked in. There were vacuum marks on the carpet.

Clearly, Ed hadn't been there all day.

The officers stared at the desk, taking it all in, before turning back to me. That's when their gaze drifted from me to the door itself, to the busted, scratched doorknob. Someone had obviously removed the knob, then reattached it.

Someone had broken in from the hall.

Shortly after, I was escorted away.

Now, when I see Regina across the laminate lunch table, I ask why she's come. Under the fluorescent lights in the visitors' center, even her delicate skin looks cantankerous. Yellow.

She feels a responsibility for me, she says. For what she did to my life. "To your children's lives." She pauses. "To Ed's." She always says the same thing. "It's the least I can do."

Finally: "Jane, I'm truly sorry."

My enemy is my last friend.

In this place I have no dreams. I thank Ed for that. Sometimes

Cheryl. But mostly my friends lithium, Lunesta, and Seroquel. After supper I dress for bed, accept my Dixie cup dosage when the nurse stops in for bed check #1. I have one hour before she returns, one hour to write down my thoughts before the meds kick in. Right on schedule, she returns for bed check #2 and dims the lights. By then, I'm beginning to drift into the shadows, my mind closing down like a city shop door at dusk, eyelids growling for the floorboards. After that there's no going back. Eight hours later the lights creep back up, and so do I. There's no night anymore. The stars fail to align. I can't remember bed checks #3, 4, and 5. The nurses sidling in with their stale breath and rubber-soled shoes.

There are signs. My bathrobe has shifted on its chair. A small plant on the sill has been turned toward the light. The vent cover is awry on its half-stripped screws. I am not the first to hide keepsakes behind it: a ChapStick, a wad of soft tissues, a small red leaf carried in on Dr. Kirkbride's shoe.

The nurses keep track of our secrets. It is part of our therapy. We should have what they call "reasonable" secrets.

But we should not have dreams. Dreams lead to unreasonable secrets. Dr. Kirkbride doesn't need to tell me that.

If I can't dream at night, I will dream in the day. A dream that is common, simple, even true. A dream of everyday life. A dream at a window over cracked concrete. The staff's collection of rusty, dinged cars. Beyond, a scruff of young trees.

A dream of supermarkets and shoe stores. Banana peppers and crabgrass plots. Of post office clerks. Dental hygienists. Cavernous, slush-filled potholes cratering lost strip-mall parking lots. The places I once spent my time, trafficking clamshelled toys and canisters of apple juice. With the kids. Their noses in an unruly state of secretion. Demanding this toy. This treat. This ride.

This. Now. Please.

Where was Ed? Nowhere to be seen. My daydream accounts for this too.

The treeless plateau outside a big-box store was heaven then. The smell of tar rising from the pavement in summer. Hot gum on the soles of my sneakers. A squeaky, broken-wheeled cart. Bobby used to ride on the back. Hanging on by one finger, hair in his eyes, he was a shoelaced peril, while the baby hiccupped and squirmed in her seat as I pushed. Her eyes on me. Always on me. Making sure I was there.

Back at the car, I strap them in. Check all the latches and belts.

"Here," I tell Bobby. "This is for you. Because you are my first, my good boy. Because you are fierce, and my joy."

He rolls his eyes. Then takes the package from my hands.

In a moment, the plastic is in his teeth. He rips and tugs—his canines have evolved for this—and eventually peels from the transparent shell a remote-controlled plane. A car that talks. A BB gun. A bow and arrow. A puppy. A personal robot. A bounce house. A battery-powered car. A rocket booster. A ray gun. My bright shining love.

The baby, meanwhile, chews on the ear of her new super-soft bunny.

Behind us, all the cars are gone. And so are the people. It's just the kids and me and a shopping cart with four new wheels on the perfectly repaved parking lot.

"Bobby," I say, looking at the cart, unbuckling him as though we've just arrived.

I don't need to say more. He's already by me, already sailing. Pumping his lean, strong legs, running and screeching and hopping on the front of the cart as it flies, his T-shirt aloft. The strip mall, our island, in the vast dark sea around us.

A sound in the hall pulls me back to Ward E. Pulls me away from these children who no longer exist. They are older now, no longer know me.

They no longer want to know me.

Children never remember their parents' care. Our delicate

footfalls. The stacks of warm washcloths. All the cool hands on fevered brows. It takes just a few years.

My children no longer remember my love.

Outside my window, a mown lawn. Trees. City houses. The lake.

On clear days, I can see all the way to Toronto. On days like today, when the sky falls and meets the gray water, I see only myself in the glass. Backlit. A smoky afternoon.

The clouds rolling up my eyes.

The halls are empty now. Many rooms are empty now. But I am here, still, roaming Ward E. A few like me remain because we cannot leave. We no longer have the will to leave. Desire takes too much energy.

I watch the construction begin. How the men shout. Re-pointing the sandstone. Resealing the floors. In the foyer, the table saws whine.

Ed is still with me. He won't leave me alone.

A marriage is always complete.

IT'S ONLY FOR FOREVER

BY TOM FONTANA

Niagara Street

This all happened a long time ago, back when Fatima's Bar and Grill was on the corner of Breckenridge and Niagara, before the joint burned to the ground. Now, I'm not saying the fire had anything to do with what happened to me. It didn't. At least, I don't think so. In any case, Fatima's is where the problem started. Problem? Catastrophe. A balls-in-your-throat catastrophe.

I was a pretty average guy before that night. Regular job, regular girlfriend with regular sex, regular apartment with regular rent, an okay car. A good life, which could have been better, but wasn't too bad. Nothing out of the ordinary.

I was at Fatima's, having a drink with Bart, my best friend for aeons, my best friend in the cosmos. I'm serious, he and I discovered the best of the best together: street hockey, chicks, deep-fried Mars bars, jerking off. He was more my blood than my brother.

That night, after a couple rounds, a couple shots of T, I told him I was going to ask Lizzie to marry me. Between shots, I'm going on and on about how much I love her, her tits, her ass, her sense of humor. The way she can manage a checkbook. And Bart's giving me major shit. But in a good way. Like best pals do.

Then I say—don't know why, maybe the booze—how much HE means to me. That I hope my marriage to Lizzie doesn't become a roadblock for him and me. Y'know, not queer or anything, but still from the heart.

He says, because he always had to one-up me, "If you got

killed tomorrow, I wouldn't be at your funeral. I'd be laying low in Mexico after killing the motherfucker who killed you. We ride together, we die together . . ."

What a mind-blowing, beautiful thing to say. I nod, "Me too . . ."

He says, "Naw, you don't mean it."

"I do. I swear, I do."

"Swear on your mother's grave."

I swore on my mother's grave. And my father's too, just for effect. But Bart was a hard nut to please. He kept shaking his head, not believing me.

He makes me write out the words on a paper napkin, then sign my name. With a cheap plastic pen, in red ink.

Then, and only then, does Bart smile. He raises his glass and we toast our undying, unconditional friendship with another shot of T.

The morning after next, the cops find Bart's body.

I call Patrice to tell her the news. Did I mention that Bart had gotten married when he was very young? A girl we went to Lafayette High School with. Her real name is Patty, but after going to France the summer between junior and senior years, she came back Patrice. Bart dug it. I thought she was a pretentious c—.

Well.

He got her preggers in the locker room at school during the senior prom and married her and they lived together in a tiny apartment over on Linwood until she threw him out because, she said, he drank too much and was too immature and had lousy friends.

But I had to let bygones be gone. Bart was dead and I figured she'd want to know. I call her and she sighs and hangs up.

Bart's father is in rehab and his mom's living in Pasadena banging some clown who owns a miniature golf course, so both parents are useless.

Which leaves me to make the funeral arrangements. Now, this was something I had never done before, because when both my parents got mangled in the car accident, my brother and my two sisters took charge, deciding this and that, everything really, including which hymns were going to be sung at the requiem Mass. I was glad about them doing that, y'know, because who wants to deal with that kinda shit?

But here I am at Amigone Funeral Home, dealing with exactly that kinda shit.

I take Lizzie with me and she's great, so loving, so supportive. I mean, I'm a basket case, right? My best friend in the whole world is a slab of meat on a cold morgue table and the cops haven't yet told me how or why he died. I'm crying nonstop, like a two-year-old on an airplane, as the amazing Lizzie and I walk into a room filled with caskets. I feel the same way I did standing in the showroom the day I bought my first car. (I got a Nissan Stanza and lived to regret it.) The undertaker, very gentle, very white-haired, talks about different kinds of woods and linings. Who knew? I'd always thought that a casket was a casket. An oblong box that people see for two, three days, then never again. Did Bart really give two shits if he was in mahogany or cypress? Shit. Maybe. How the fuck would I know?

The undertaker drones on, asking about flowers and funeral cards and limos and . . .

Lord God in heaven, I have to make choices (silk or satin inside the box) and I have to make them fast, but my brain is in some weird vapor lock or something.

Then Lizzie says—this is why I loved her, why I always will—"Honey, pick any coffin, any lining. It's only for forever."

I laugh. We go back to my place and fuck in the bathroom. Wait. Why am I'm telling you this part? It's got nothing to do with the rest.

While I'm dealing with the details for the wake and the burial and the "reception" (at Fatima's) afterward, the cops are supposedly investigating. But they have no clues, no evidence, no witnesses, no, no, no, no, no. They release the body from the morgue and the undertaker paints it up to look almost human and we plant Bart in the ground like a petunia, over at Mount Calvary, near the expressway.

Rest in peace. If you like the sound of traffic.

By this point, the fucking cops rule Bart's death a suicide, a self-inflicted gunshot wound to the heart. Bullshit. Even I know he couldn't have held the gun that far from his chest for the trajectory to work. Buffalo PD. Lazy fucks. (Okay, not all of them: once this uniform, a black guy, got my bicycle back from some asshole junkie.)

I head over, with Lizzie, to Bart's apartment to clear out his stuff. I am amazed at how neat the place is. Bart was not, by nature, neat. But even his bed is made. Almost as if Bart knew he wasn't coming back.

We give most of his belongings to the Salvation Army. There wasn't much, I mean, he wasn't some Saudi prince. I kept his catcher's mitt and a cashmere scarf that I'd always coveted. I sent his dad an old family photo of the three of them at Allegheny State Park. I sent Bart's mom a set of salt and pepper shakers that he'd bought when he was twelve on a trip with his Catholic Academy class to New York City. I never heard back from either of them. Not that I expected a thank you. I wasn't doing this for them.

Oh, and Bart had an overdue library book, Hunter Thompson fearing and loathing something, which I return and pay the fine. I didn't even know that Bart had a library card. Who still has a library card?

On the way back home, on an impulse, I drive over to Broderick Park. I want to see the spot where Bart died. The yellow crime scene tape had snapped and flapped in an angry wind. On the grass is a trickle of blood. I light a cigarette and stand there until the sun disappears, sinking behind the Peace Bridge.

* * *

The next Tuesday, I'm oversleeping, my alarm clock in pieces on other side of the bedroom, when I get a call from a lawyer, Mickey Greene, saying that I'd been left something in Bart's will. Bart had a will? Bart had a lawyer? Right then, right there, I should have known that something was fucked, that I was fucked.

That afternoon, I arrive at the offices of Greene, Muscarella, and Jefferson. Mickey Greene, who looks about twelve and speaks really fast, hands me an envelope, with the words *TO BE OPENED AT MY DEATH* scrawled on the front in red marker.

Red. Sure. Bart had a sense of humor, though I didn't realize the joke until I tore open the envelope.

Inside was a US passport for a guy I'd never heard of. And, folded in half, a paper napkin with the words, *If you got killed tomorrow, I wouldn't be at your funeral. I'd be laying low in Mexico after killing the motherfucker who killed you. We ride together, we die together.* And at the bottom, my fucking signature.

Yeah, you got it.

Oh, sure, of course, before I do anything, I take the passport to the cops and tell them that this fat, bald guy in the passport, name of Rolin Rivers, might have something to do with Bart's untimely demise. That Bart had left an envelope for me, *TO BE OPENED AT MY DEATH*. Naturally, I don't mention the napkin.

I'm insistent that they at least talk to this joker Rivers. I'm insistent because of what's at stake: justice for Bart and—fuck me—the promise I'd made, which I did not want to fulfill. Finally, the cops say they'll interview Rivers. They practically shove me out the door. In their defense, Bart's was the second suspicious death in two weeks and the department was getting plenty of heat.

I wait and wait for the phone to ring. I gotta admit, by this point my nerves are rattled. I'm starting to get yelled at a lot at work. Lizzie seems constantly pissed off at me. I'm waking up at Fatima's, at dawn, facedown on a table of dried beer and potato chip shards. Christ, the stench of the human body, alive or dead.

Days later, having still not heard a word from the cops, I go back to the homicide unit. Yes, they'd interviewed the guy whose face was on the passport, Rolin Rivers, but he had an alibi for the night Bart died. He was at a Bills game with the pastor of his church. (He was Episcopalian. Catholicism without the guilt.)

"Did you talk to the pastor?" I ask.

"Sure, he confirmed that they were together the whole time."

"The whole time? Rolin Rivers never went to buy a soda or take a piss?"

"Even if he had, how fast could he have gotten from the stadium all the way to Broderick Park and back without the good reverend noticing?"

"Okay," I say, "but Rivers could have hired someone to shoot—"

One of the detectives, a barrel-chested goon with brown teeth, suddenly giggles in a girlish way, "You watch too much TV."

Yeah, you got it, you know what's next.

I track down Rolin Rivers in Getzville. I study his every move, morning to midnight. I wait, with the calm of a Vegas card dealer shuffling a deck. I wait until one evening when Rivers is leaving his house. I'm in the garage when he slides his fat ass into the driver's seat. I make him drive me to Broderick Park, to the spot of green grass. I tie him up. I light a cigarette, an American Spirit, and use the edge to burn his pale, sweaty skin until he talks.

Boy, does he talk. I can't shut the bastard up. He babbles, like a car without brakes, about what Bart had done and why Rivers hated him and why he'd had Bart killed. I'm not going into the specifics, but let me just say that the guy Rivers described was not Bart. No way. Not my best friend. Not my brother in life. Rivers was wrong, he had the wrong guy. I'd known Bart since the beginning of time. No way.

I'm well aware that the confession Rivers has made to me is inadmissible in court (yeah, too much TV) and that, if I let him go, I'll be the one facing prison time.

Shit, in for a penny, in for a pound.

I pull a car jack out of the trunk of the Chevy. I swing. There's a lotta fucking blood. And a lotta silence.

I walk away, slowly, in a daze. I do remember dropping the car jack into the canal. And wondering whether I should find the guy who had actually fired the bullet into Bart's heart. A professional hit man or some local punk? Either way, I decide, I've done enough. I've killed the man responsible. This is all the justice that friendship requires.

I stop at a 7-Eleven for a Slurpie, but there's a look of fright in the cashier's eyes. Blood on my hands, on my face. I run out and keep running, down the street, stripping off my clothes. In my apartment, I take a shower and change into a fresh tee and jeans. I throw some crap into a gym bag. I call Lizzie, but get her voice mail.

She was at a movie with Allison Carmichael. Some Brad Pitt chick thing.

I leave a message saying that I called, but that it wasn't important and I'd phone her later and "I love you . . ."

I climb into my car and drive. I drive as fast as I can. I drive into darkness. All the while thinking about Lizzie. And Bart.

A promise is a promise, right? A friend is a friend, in good times and the worst times. Like a wife. And so, you do what you have to do.

Words on a paper napkin.

Now I'm living here in Playa de los Muertos. A tour guide for fat, bald Americans. With a wife named Rosalina. A small house on the beach. An okay car.

Every day, as the sun goes down, I toast my best friend Bart with a shot of T.

THE EHRENGRAF SETTLEMENT

BY LAWRENCE BLOCK

Nottingham Terrace

Ehrengraf, his mind abuzz with uplifting thoughts, left his car at the curb and walked the length of the flagstone path to Millard Ravenstock's imposing front door. There was a large bronze door knocker in the shape of an elephant's head, and one could lift and lower the animal's hinged proboscis to summon the occupants.

Or, as an alternative, one could ring the doorbell by pressing the recessed mother-of-pearl button. Ehrengraf fingered the knot in his tie, with its alternating half-inch stripes of scarlet and Prussian blue, brushed a speck of lint from the lapel of his gray flannel suit. Only then, having given both choices due consideration, did he touch the elephant's trunk, before opting instead for the bell-push.

Moments later he was in a paneled library, seated in a leather club chair, with a cup of coffee at hand. He hadn't managed more than two sips before Millard Ravenstock joined him.

"Mr. Ehrengraf," the man said, giving the honorific just enough emphasis to suggest how rarely he employed it. Ehrengraf could believe it; this was a man who would call most people by their surnames, as if all the world's inhabitants were members of his household staff.

"Mr. Ravenstock," said Ehrengraf, with an inflection that was similar but not identical.

"It was good of you to come to see me. In ordinary circumstances I'd have called at your offices, but—" A shrug and a smile served to complete the sentence.

In ordinary circumstances, Ehrengraf thought, there'd have been no need for their paths to cross. Had Millard Ravenstock not found himself a person of interest in a murder investigation, he'd have had no reason to summon Ehrengraf, or Ehrengraf any reason to come to the imposing Nottingham Terrace residence.

Ehrengraf simply observed that the circumstances were not ordinary.

"Indeed they are not," said Ravenstock. His chalk-striped navy suit was clearly the work of a custom tailor, who'd shown skill in flattering his client's physique. Ravenstock was an imposing figure, stout enough to draw a physician's perfunctory warnings about cholesterol and type 2 diabetes, but still well on the right side of the current national standard for obesity. Ehrengraf, who maintained an ideal weight with no discernible effort, rather agreed with Shakespeare's Caesar, liking to have men about him who were fat.

"Sleek-headed men, and such as sleep a-nights."

"I beg your pardon?"

Had he spoken aloud? Ehrengraf smiled, and waved a dismissive hand. "Perhaps," he said, "we should consider the matter that concerns us."

"Tegrum Bogue," Ravenstock said, pronouncing the name with distaste. "What kind of a name is Tegrum Bogue?"

"A distinctive one," Ehrengraf suggested.

"Distinctive if not distinguished. I've no quarrel with the surname. One assumes it came down to him from the man who provided half his DNA. But why would anyone name a child Tegrum? With all the combinations of letters available, why pick those six and arrange them in that order?" He frowned. "Never mind, I'm wandering off topic. What does his name matter? What's relevant is that I'm about to be charged with his murder."

"They allege that you shot him."

"And the allegation is entirely true," Ravenstock said. "I don't suppose you like to hear me admit as much, Mr. Ehrengraf.

But it's pointless for me to deny it, because it's the plain and simple truth."

Ehrengraf, whose free time was largely devoted to the reading of poetry, moved from Shakespeare to Oscar Wilde, who had pointed out that the truth was rarely plain, and never simple. But he kept himself from quoting aloud.

"It was self-defense," Ravenstock said. "The man was hanging around my property and behaving suspiciously. I confronted him. He responded in a menacing fashion. I urged him to depart. He attacked me. Then and only then did I draw my pistol and shoot him dead."

"Ah," said Ehrengraf.

"It was quite clear that I was blameless." Ravenstock's high forehead was dry, but he drew a handkerchief and mopped it just the same. "The police questioned me, as they were unquestionably right to do, and released me, and one detective said offhand that I'd done the right thing. I consulted with my attorney, and he said he doubted charges would be brought, but that if they were he was confident of a verdict of justifiable homicide."

"And then things began to go wrong."

"Horribly wrong, Mr. Ehrengraf. But you probably know the circumstances as well as I do."

"I try to keep up," Ehrengraf allowed. "But let me confirm a few facts. You're a member of the Nottingham Vigilance Committee."

"The name's unfortunate," Ravenstock said. "It simply identifies the group as what it is, designed to keep a watchful eye over our neighborhood. This is an affluent area, and right across the street is Delaware Park. That's one of the best things about living here, but it's not an unmixed blessing."

"Few blessings are," said Ehrengraf.

"I'll have to think about that. But the park—it's beautiful, it's convenient, and at the same time people lurk there, some of them criminous, some of them emotionally disturbed, and all of them just a stone's throw from our houses."

There was a remark that was trying to occur to Ehrengraf, something about glass houses, but he left it unsaid.

"Police protection is good here," Ravenstock continued, "but there's a definite need for a neighborhood watch group. Vigilance— well, you hear that and you think *vigilante*, don't you?"

"One does. This Mr. Bogue—"

"Tegrum Bogue."

"Tegrum Bogue. You'd had confrontations with him before."

"I'd seen him on my property once or twice," Ravenstock said, "and warned him off."

"You'd called in reports of his suspicious behavior to the police."

"A couple of times, yes."

"And on the night in question," Ehrengraf said, "he was not actually on your property. He was, as I understand it, two doors away."

"In front of the Gissling home. Heading north toward Meadow Road, there's this house, and then the Robert Townsend house, and then Madge and Bernard Gissling's. So that would be two doors away."

"And when you shot him, he fell dead on the Gisslings' lawn."

"They'd just resodded."

"That very day?"

"No, a month ago. Why?"

Ehrengraf smiled, a maneuver that had served him well over the years. "Mr. Bogue—that would be Tegrum Bogue—was unarmed."

"He had a knife in his pocket."

"An inch-long penknife, wasn't it? Attached to his key ring?"

"I couldn't say, sir. I never saw the knife. The police report mentioned it. It was only an inch long?"

"Apparently."

"It doesn't sound terribly formidable, does it? But Bogue's was a menacing presence without a weapon in evidence. He was young and tall and vigorous and muscular and wild-eyed, and he uttered threats and put his hands on me and pushed me and struck me."

"You were armed."

"An automatic pistol, made by Gunnar & Swick. Their Kestrel model. It's registered, and I'm licensed to carry it."

"You drew your weapon."

"I did. I thought the sight of it might stop Bogue in his tracks."

"But it didn't."

"He laughed," Ravenstock recalled, "and said he'd take it away from me, and would stick it—well, you can imagine where he threatened to stick it."

Ehrengraf, who could actually imagine several possible destinations for the Kestrel, simply nodded.

"And he rushed at me, and I might have been holding a water pistol for all the respect he showed it."

"You fired it."

"I was taught never to show a gun unless I was prepared to use it."

"Five times."

"I was taught to keep on firing until one's gun is empty. Actually, the Kestrel's clip holds nine cartridges, but five seemed sufficient."

"*To make assurance doubly sure*," Ehrengraf said. "Stopping at five does show restraint."

"Well."

"And yet," Ehrengraf said, "the traditional argument that the gun simply went off of its own accord comes a cropper, doesn't it? It's a rare weapon that fires itself five times in rapid succession. As a member of the Nottingham Vigilantes—"

"The Vigilance Committee."

"Yes, of course. In that capacity, weren't you supposed to report Bogue's presence to the police rather than confront him?"

Ravenstock came as close to hanging his head as his character would allow. "I never thought to make the call."

"The heat of the moment," Ehrengraf offered.

"Just that. I acted precipitously."

"A Mrs. Kling was across the street, walking her Gordon setter. She told police the two of you were arguing, and it seemed to be about someone's wife."

"He made remarks about my wife," Ravenstock said. "Brutish remarks, designed to provoke me. About what he intended to do to and with her, after he'd taken the gun away from me and put it, well—"

"Indeed."

"What's worse, Mr. Ehrengraf, is the campaign of late to canonize Tegrum Bogue. Have you seen the picture his family released to the press? He doesn't look very menacing, does he?"

"Only if one finds choirboys threatening."

"It was taken nine years ago," Ravenstock said, "when young Bogue was a first-form student at the Nichols School. Since then he shot up eight inches and put on forty or fifty pounds. I assure you, the cherub in the photo bears no resemblance to the hulking savage who attacked me steps from my own home."

"Unconscionable," Ehrengraf said.

"And now I'm certain to be questioned further, and very likely to be placed under arrest. My lawyer was nattering on about how unlikely it is that I'd ever have to spend a night in jail, and hinting at my pleading guilty to some reduced charge. That's not good enough."

"No."

"I don't want to skate on a technicality, my reputation in ruins. I don't want to devote a few hundred hours to community service. How do you suppose they'd have me serve my community, Mr. Ehrengraf? Would they send me across the street to pick up litter in the park? Or would they regard a stick with a sharp bit of metal at its end as far too formidable a weapon to be placed in my irresponsible hands?"

"These are things you don't want," Ehrengraf said soothingly. "And why ever should you want them? But perhaps you could tell me what it is you *do* want."

"What I want," said Ravenstock, speaking as a man who generally gets whatever it is that he wants. "What I want, sir, is for all of this to go away. And my understanding is that you are a gentleman who is very good at making things go away."

Ehrengraf smiled.

Ehrengraf gazed past the mound of clutter on his desk at his office door, with its window of frosted glass. What struck him about the door was that his client had not yet come through it. It was getting on for half past eleven, which made Millard Ravenstock almost thirty minutes late.

Ehrengraf fingered the knot in his tie. It was a perfectly symmetrical knot, neither too large nor too small, which was as it should be. Whenever he wore this particular tie, with its navy field upon which a half-inch diagonal stripe of royal blue was flanked by two narrower stripes, one of gold, the other vividly green—whenever he put it on, he took considerable pains to get the knot exactly right.

It was, of course, the tie of the Caedmon Society; Ehrengraf, not a member of that institution, had purchased the tie from a shop in Oxford's Cranham Close. He'd owned it for some years now, and had been careful to avoid soiling it, extending its useful life by reserving it for special occasions.

This morning had promised to be such an occasion. Now, as the minutes ticked away without producing Millard Ravenstock, he found himself less certain.

The antique regulator clock on the wall, which lost a minute a day, showed the time as 11:42 when Millard Ravenstock

LAWRENCE BLOCK // 53

opened the door and stepped into Ehrengraf's office. The little lawyer glanced first at the clock and then at his wristwatch, which read 11:48. Then he looked at his client, who appeared not the least bit apologetic for his late arrival.

"Ah, Ehrengraf," the man said. "A fine day, wouldn't you say?"

You could see Niagara Square from the office window, and a quick look showed that the day was as it had been earlier— overcast and gloomy, with every likelihood of rain.

"Glorious," Ehrengraf agreed.

Without waiting to be asked, Ravenstock pulled up a chair and settled his bulk into it. "Before I left my house," he said, "I went into my den, got out my checkbook, and wrote two checks. One, you'll be pleased to know, was for your fee." He patted his breast pocket. "I've brought it with me."

Ehrengraf was pleased. But, he noted, cautiously so. He sensed there was another shoe just waiting to be dropped.

"The other check is already in the mail. I made it payable to the Policemen's Benevolent Association, and I assure you the sum is a generous one. I have always been a staunch proponent of the police, Ehrengraf, if only because the role they play is such a vital one. Without them we'd have the rabble at our throats, eh?"

Ehrengraf, thought Ehrengraf. The *Mister,* present throughout their initial meeting, had evidently been left behind on Nottingham Terrace. Increasingly, he felt it had been an error to wear that particular tie on this particular morning.

"Yet I'd given the police insufficient credit for their insight and their resolve. Walter Bainbridge, a thorough and diligent policeman and, I might add, a good friend, pressed an investigation along lines others might have left unexplored. I've been completely exonerated, and it's largely his doing."

"Indeed," said Ehrengraf.

"The police dug up evidence, unearthed facts. That housewife who was raped and murdered three weeks ago in Orchard

Park. I'm sure you're familiar with the case. The press called it the Milf Murder."

Ehrengraf nodded.

"It took place outside city limits," Ravenstock continued, "so it wasn't their case at all, but they went through the house and found an unwashed sweatshirt stuffed into a trash can in the garage. *Nichols School Lacrosse*, it said, big as life. That's a curious expression, isn't it? Big as life?"

"Curious," Ehrengraf said.

"Lacrosse seems to be the natural refuge of the preppy thug," Ravenstock said. "Can you guess whose DNA soiled that sweatshirt?"

Ehrengraf could guess, but saw no reason to do so. Nor did Ravenstock wait for a response.

"Tegrum Bogue's. He'd been on the team, and it was beyond question his shirt. He'd raped that young housewife and snapped her neck when he was through with her. And he had similar plans for Alicia."

"Your wife."

"Yes. I don't believe you've met her."

"I haven't had the pleasure."

The expression that passed over Ravenstock's face suggested that it was a pleasure Ehrengraf would have to live without. "She is a beautiful woman," he said. "And quite a few years younger than I. I suppose there are those who would refer to her as my trophy wife." The man paused, waiting for Ehrengraf to comment, then frowned at the lawyer's continuing silence. "There are two ways to celebrate a trophy," he went on. "One may carry it around, showing it off at every opportunity. Or one may place it on a shelf in one's personal quarters, to be admired and savored in private."

"Indeed."

"Some men require that their taste have the approbation of others. They lack confidence, Ehrengraf."

Another pause. Some expression of assent seemed to be required of him, and Ehrengraf considered several, ranging from *Right on, dude* to *Most def.* "Indeed," he said again at length.

"But somehow Alicia caught his interest. He was one of the mob given to loitering in the park, and sometimes she'd walk Kossuth there."

"Kossuth," Ehrengraf said. "The Gordon setter?"

"No, of course not. I wouldn't own a Gordon. And why would anyone name a Gordon for Louis Kossuth? Our dog is a vizsla, and a fine and noble animal he is. He must have seen her walking Kossuth. Or . . ."

"Or?"

"I had my run-ins with him. In my patrol duty with the Vigilance Committee, I'd recommended that he and his fellows stay on their side of the street."

"In the park, and away from the houses."

"His response was not at all acquiescent," Ravenstock recalled. "After that I made a point of monitoring his activities, and phoned in the occasional police report. I'd have to say I made an enemy, Ehrengraf."

"I doubt you were ever destined to be friends."

"No, but I erred in making myself the object of his hostility. I think that's what may have put Alicia in his sights. I think he stalked me, and I think his reconnaissance got him a good look at Alicia, and of course to see her is to want her."

Ehrengraf, struck by the matter-of-fact tone of that last clause, touched the tips of two fingers to the Caedmon Society cravat.

"And the police found evidence of his obsession," Ravenstock said. "A roll of undeveloped film in his sock drawer, with photos for which my wife had served as an unwitting model. Crude fictional sketches, written in Bogue's schoolboy hand, some written in the third person, some in the first. Clumsy ministries relating in pornographic detail the abduction, sexual savaging, and murder of my wife. Pencil drawings to illustrate them, as ill-fashioned as his prose. The scenarios varied as his fantasies evolved. Sometimes there was torture, mutilation, dismemberment. Sometimes I was present, bound and helpless, forced to witness what was being done to her. And I had to watch because I couldn't close my eyes. I didn't read his filth, so I can't recall whether he'd glued my eyelids open or removed them surgically—"

"Either would be effective."

"Well," Ravenstock said, and explained that of course the several discoveries the police had made put paid to any notion that he, Millard Ravenstock, had done anything untoward, let alone criminal. He had not been charged, so there were no charges to dismiss, and what was at least as important was that he had been entirely exonerated in the court of public opinion. "So you can see why I felt moved to make a generous donation to the Policemen's Benevolent Association. I feel they earned it. And I'll find a way to express my private appreciation to Walter Bainbridge."

Ehrengraf waited, and refrained from touching his necktie.

"As for yourself, Ehrengraf, I greatly appreciate your efforts on my behalf, and have no doubt that they'd have proved successful had not Fate and the police intervened and done your job for you. And I'm sure you'll find this more than adequate compensation for your good work."

The check was in an envelope, which Ravenstock plucked from his inside breast pocket and extended with a flourish. The envelope was unsealed, and Ehrengraf drew the check from it and noted its amount, which was about what he'd come to expect.

"The fee I quoted you—"

"Was lofty," Ravenstock said, "but would have been acceptable had the case not resolved itself independent of any action on your part."

"I was very specific," Ehrengraf pointed out. "I said my work would cost you nothing unless your innocence was established and all charges dropped. But if that were to come about, my fee was due and payable in full. You do remember my saying that, don't you?"

"But you didn't *do* anything, Ehrengraf."

"You agreed to the arrangement I spelled out, sir, and—"

"I repeat, you did nothing, or if you did do anything it had no bearing on the outcome of the matter. The payment I just gave you is a settlement, and I pay it gladly in order to put the matter to rest."

"A settlement," Ehrengraf said, testing the word on his tongue.

"And no mere token settlement, either. It's hardly an insignificant amount, and my personal attorney hastened to tell me I'm being overly generous. He says all you're entitled to, legally and morally, is a reasonable return on whatever billable hours you've put in, and—"

"Your attorney."

"One of the region's top men, I assure you."

"I don't doubt it. Would this be the same attorney who'd have had you armed with a sharp stick to pick up litter in Delaware Park? After pleading you guilty to a murder for which you bore no guilt?"

Even as he marshaled his arguments, Ehrengraf sensed that they would prove fruitless. The man's mind, such as it was, was made up. Nothing would sway him.

There was a time, Ehrengraf recalled, when he had longed for a house like Millard Ravenstock's—on Nottingham Terrace, or Meadow Road, or Middlesex. Something at once tasteful and baronial, something with pillars and a center hall, something that would proclaim to one and all that its owner had unquestionably come to amount to something.

True success, he had learned, meant one no longer required its accoutrements. His penthouse apartment on Park Lane provided all the space and luxury he could want, and a better view than any house could offer. The building, immaculately maintained and impeccably staffed, even had a name that suited him; it managed to be as resolutely British as Nottingham or Middlesex without sounding pretentious.

And it was closer to downtown. When time and good weather permitted, Ehrengraf could walk to and from his office.

But not today. There was a cold wind blowing off the lake, and the handicappers in the weather bureau had pegged rain at even money. The little lawyer had arrived at his office a few minutes after ten. He made one phone call, and as he rang off he realized he could have saved himself the trip.

He went downstairs, retrieved his car, and returned to Park Lane to await his guest.

Ehrengraf, opening the door, was careful not to stare. The woman whom the concierge had announced as a Ms. Philips was stunning, and Ehrengraf worked to conceal the extent to which he was stunned. She was taller than Ehrengraf by several inches, with dark hair that someone very skilled had cut to look as though she took no trouble with it. She had great big Bambi eyes, the facial planes of a supermodel, and a full-lipped mouth that stopped just short of obscenity.

"Ms. Philips," Ehrengraf said, and motioned her inside.

"I didn't want to leave my name at the desk."

"I assumed as much. Come in, come in. A drink? A cup of coffee?"

"Coffee, if it's no trouble."

It was no trouble at all, Ehrengraf had made a fresh pot upon his return, and he filled two cups and brought them to the living room, where Alicia Ravenstock had chosen the Sheraton wing chair. Ehrengraf sat opposite her, and they sipped their coffee and discussed the beans and brewing method before giving a few minutes' attention to the weather.

Then she said, "You're very good to see me here. I was afraid to come to your office. There are enough people who know me by sight, and if word got back to him that I went to a lawyer's office, or even into a building where lawyers had offices—"

"I can imagine."

"I'm his alone, you see. I can have anything I want, except the least bit of freedom."

"Peter, Peter, pumpkin eater," Ehrengraf said, and when she looked puzzled he quoted the rhyme in full:

Peter, Peter, pumpkin eater,
Had a wife and couldn't keep her.
He put her in a pumpkin shell
And there he kept her very well.

"Yes, of course. It's a nursery rhyme, isn't it?"

Ehrengraf nodded. "I believe it began life centuries ago as satirical political doggerel, but it's lived on as a rhyme for children."

"Millard keeps me very well," she said. "You've been to the pumpkin shell, haven't you? It's a very elegant one."

"It is."

"A sumptuous and comfortable prison. I suppose I shouldn't complain. It's what I wanted. Or what I thought I wanted, which may amount to the same thing. I'd resigned myself to it—or *thought* I'd resigned myself to it."

"Which may amount to the same thing."

"Yes," she said, and took a sip of coffee. "And then I met Bo."

"And that would be Tegrum Bogue."

"I thought we were careful," she said. "I never had any intimation that Millard knew, or even suspected." Her face clouded. "He was a lovely boy, you know. It's still hard for me to believe he's gone."

"And that your husband killed him."

"That part's not difficult to believe," she said. "Millard's cold as ice and harder than stone. The part I can't understand is how someone like him could care enough to want me."

"You're a possession," Ehrengraf suggested.

"Yes, of course. There's no other explanation." Another sip of coffee; Ehrengraf, watching her mouth, found himself envying the bone china cup. "It wouldn't have lasted," she said. "I was too old for Bo, even as Millard is too old for me. Mr. Ehrengraf, I had resigned myself to living the life Millard wanted me to live. Then Bo came along, and a sunbeam brightened up my prison cell, so to speak, and the life to which I'd resigned myself was now transformed into one I could enjoy."

"Made so by trysts with your young lover."

"Trysts," she said. "I like the word, it sounds permissibly naughty. But, you know, it also sounds like *tristesse*, which is sadness in French."

A woman who cared about words was very likely a woman on whom the charms of poetry would not be lost. Ehrengraf found himself wishing he'd quoted something rather more distinguished than *Peter, Peter, pumpkin eater*.

"I don't know how Millard found out about Bo," she said. "Or how he contrived to face him mere steps from our house and shoot him down like a dog. But there seemed to be no question of his guilt, and I assumed he'd have to answer in some small way for what he'd done. He wouldn't go to prison, rich men never do, but look at him now, Mr. Ehrengraf, proclaimed a defender of home and hearth who slew a rapist and murderer. To think that a sweet and gentle boy like Bo could have his reputation so blackened. It's heartbreaking."

"There, there," Ehrengraf said, and patted the back of her hand. The skin was remarkably soft, and it felt at once both warm and cool, which struck him as an insoluble paradox but one worth investigating. "There, there," he said again, but omitted the pat this time.

"I blame the police. Millard donates to their fund-raising efforts and wields influence on their behalf, and I'd say it paid off for him."

Ehrengraf listed while Alicia Ravenstock speculated on just how the police, led by a man named Bainbridge, might have constructed a postmortem frame for Tegrum Bogue. She had, he was pleased to note, an incisive imagination. When she'd finished he suggested more coffee, and she shook her head.

"I have to end my marriage," she said abruptly. "There's nothing for it. I made a bad bargain, and for a time I thought I could live with it, and now I see the impossibility of so doing."

"A divorce, Mrs. Ravenstock . . ."

She recoiled at the name, then forced a smile. "Please don't call me that," she said. "I don't like being reminded that it's my name. Call me Alicia, Mr. Ehrengraf."

"Then you must call me Martin, Alicia."

"Martin," she said, testing the name on her pink tongue.

"It's not terribly difficult to obtain a divorce, Alicia. But of course you would know that. And you would know, too, that a specialist in matrimonial law would best serve your interests, and you wouldn't come to me seeing a recommendation in that regard."

She smiled, letting him find his way.

"A prenuptial agreement," he said. "He insisted you sign one and you did."

"Yes."

"And you've shown it to an attorney, who pronounced it ironclad."

"Yes."

"You don't want more coffee. But would you have a cordial? Benedictine? Chartreuse? Perhaps a Drambuie?"

"It's a Scotch-based liqueur," Ehrengraf said, after his guest had sampled her drink and signified her approval.

"I've never had it before, Martin. It's very nice."

"More appropriate as an after-dinner drink, some might say. But it brightens an afternoon, especially one with weather that might have swept in from the Scottish Highlands." He might have quoted Robert Burns, but nothing came to mind. "Alicia," he said, "I made a great mistake when I agreed to act as your husband's attorney. I violated one of my own cardinal principles. I have made a career of representing the innocent, the blameless, the unjustly accused. When I am able to believe in a client's innocence, no matter how damning the apparent evidence of his guilt, then I feel justified in committing myself unreservedly to his defense."

"And if you can't believe him to be innocent?"

"Then I decline the case." A sigh escaped the lawyer's lips. "Your husband admitted his guilt. He seemed quite unrepentant, he asserted his moral right to act as he had done. And, because at the time I could see some justification for his behavior, I enlisted in his service." He set his jaw. "Perhaps it's just as well that he declined to pay the fee upon which we'd agreed."

"He boasted about that, Martin." How sweet his name sounded on those plump lips!

"Did he indeed."

"*I gave him a tenth of what he wanted*, he said, *and he was lucky to get anything at all from me*. Of course he wasn't just bragging, he was letting me know just how tightfisted I could expect him to be."

"Yes, he'd have that in mind."

"You asked if I'd shown the prenup to an attorney. I had trouble finding one who'd look at it, or even let me into his office. What I discovered was that Millard had consulted every matrimonial lawyer within a radius of five hundred miles. He'd had each of them review the agreement and spend five minutes discussing it with him, and as a result they were ethically enjoined from representing me."

"For perhaps a thousand dollars a man, he'd made it impossible for you to secure representation." Ehrengraf frowned. "He did all this after discovering about you and young Bogue?"

"He began these consultations when we returned from our honeymoon."

"Had your discontent already become evident?"

"Not even to me, Martin. Millard was simply taking precautions." She finished her Drambuie, set down the empty glass. "And I did find a lawyer, a young man with a general practice, who took a look at the agreement I'd signed. He kept telling me it wasn't his area of expertise. But he said it looked rock-solid to him."

"Ah," said Ehrengraf. "Well, we'll have to see about that, won't we?"

It was three weeks and a day later when Ehrengraf emerged from his morning shower and toweled himself dry. He shaved, and spent a moment or two trimming a few errant hairs from his beard, a Vandyke that came to a precise point.

Beards had come and gone in Ehrengraf's life, and upon his chin, and he felt this latest incarnation was the most successful to date. There was just the least hint of gray in it, even as there was the slightest touch of gray at his temples.

He hoped it would stay that way, at least for a while. With gray, as with so many things, a little was an asset, a lot a liability. One couldn't successfully command time to stand still, any more than King Canute could order a cessation of the tidal flow. There would be more gray, and the day would come when he would either accept it (and, by implication, all the slings and arrows of the aging process) or reach for the bottle of hair coloring.

Neither prospect was appealing. But both were off in the future, and did not bear thinking about. Certainly not on what was to be a day of triumph, a triumph all the sweeter for having been delayed.

He took his time dressing, choosing his newest suit, a three-piece navy pinstripe from Peller & Mure. He considered several shirts and settled on a spread-collar broadcloth in French blue, not least of all for the way it would complement his tie.

And the choice of tie was foreordained. It was, of course, that of the Caedmon Society.

The spread collar called for a double Windsor, and Ehrengraf's fingers were equal to the task. He slipped his feet into black monk-strap loafers, then considered the suit's third piece, the vest. The only argument against it was that it would conceal much of his tie, but the tie and its significance were important only to the wearer.

He decided to go with the vest.

And now? It was getting on toward nine, and his appointment was at his office, at half past ten. He'd had his light breakfast, and the day was clear and bright and neither too warm nor too cold. He could walk to his office, taking his time, stopping along the way for a cup of coffee.

But why not wait and see if the phone might chance to ring?

And it did, just after nine o'clock. Ehrengraf smiled when it rang, and his smile broadened at the sound of the caller's voice, and broadened further as he listened. "Yes, of course," he said. "I'd like that."

"When we spoke yesterday," Alicia Ravenstock said, "I automatically suggested a meeting at your office. Because I'd been uncomfortable going there before, and now the reason for that discomfort had been removed."

"So you wanted to exercise your new freedom."

"Then I remembered what a nice apartment you have, and what good coffee I enjoyed on my previous visit."

"When you called," Ehrengraf said, "the first thing I did was make a fresh pot."

He fetched a cup for each of them, and watched her purse her lips and take a first sip.

"Just right," she said. "There's so much to talk about, Martin, but I'd like to get the business part out of the way."

She drew an envelope from her purse, and Ehrengraf held his breath, at least metaphorically, while he opened it. This was the second time he'd received an envelope from someone with Ravenstock for a surname, and the first time had proved profoundly disappointing.

Still, she'd used his first name, and moved their meeting from his office to his residence. Those ought to be favorable omens.

The check, he saw at a glance, had the correct number of zeroes. His eyes widened when he took a second look at it. "This is higher than the sum we agreed on," he said.

"By 10 percent. I've suddenly become a wealthy woman, Martin, and I felt a bonus was in order. I hope you don't regard it as an insult . . ."

Money? An insult? He assured her that it was nothing of the sort.

"It's really quite remarkable," she said. "Millard is in jail, where he's being held without bail. I've filed suit for divorce, and my attorney assures me that the prenup is essentially null and void. Martin, I knew the evidence against Bo was bogus. But I had no idea it would all come to light as it has."

"It was an interesting chain of events," he agreed.

"It was a tissue of lies," she said, "and it started to unravel when someone called Channel 7's investigative reporter, pointing out that Bo was at a hockey game when the Milf Murder took place. How could he be in two places at the same time?"

"How indeed?"

"And then there was the damning physical evidence, the lacrosse shirt with Bo's DNA. They found a receipt among the boy's effects for a bag of clothes donated to Goodwill Industries, and among the several items mentioned was one Nichols School lacrosse jersey. How Millard knew about the donation and got his hands on the shirt—"

"We may never know, Alicia. And it may not have been Millard himself who found the shirt."

"It was probably Bainbridge. But we won't know that, either, now that he's dead."

"Suicide is a terrible thing," Ehrengraf said. "And sometimes it seems to ask as many questions as it answers. Though this particular act did answer quite a few."

"Walter Bainbridge was Millard's closest friend in the police department, and I thought it was awfully convenient the way he came up with all the evidence against Bo. But I guess Channel 7's investigation convinced him he'd gone too far, and when the truth about the lacrosse shirt came to light, he could see the walls closing in. How desperate he must have been to put his service revolver in his mouth and blow his brains out."

"It was more than the evidence he faked. The note he left suggests he himself may have committed the Milf Murder. You see, it's almost certain he committed a similar rape and murder in Kenmore just days before he took his own life."

"The nurse," she remembered. "There was no physical evidence at the crime scene, but his note alluded to 'other bad things I've done,' and didn't they find something of hers in Bainbridge's desk at police headquarters?"

"A pair of soiled panties."

"The pervert. So he had ample reason to pin the Milf Murder on Bo. To help Millard, and to divert any possible suspicion from himself. This really is superb coffee."

"May I bring you a fresh cup?"

"Not quite yet, Martin. Those notebooks of Bo's, with the crude drawings and the fantasies? They seemed so unlikely to me, so much at variance with the Tegrum Bogue I knew."

"They've turned out to be forgeries."

"Rather skillful forgeries," she said, "but forgeries all the same. Bainbridge had imitated Bo's handwriting, and he'd left behind a notebook in which he'd written out drafts of the material in his own hand, then practiced copying them in Bo's. And do you know what else they found?"

"Something of your husband's, I believe."

"Millard supplied those fantasies for Bainbridge. He wrote them out in his own cramped hand, and gave them to Bainbridge to save his policeman friend the necessity of using his imagination. But before he did this he made photocopies, which he kept. They turned up in a strongbox in his closet, and they were a perfect match for the originals that had been among Bainbridge's effects."

"Desperate men do desperate things. I'm sure he denies everything."

"Of course. It won't do him any good. The police came out of this looking very bad, and it's no help to blame Walter Bainbridge, as he's beyond their punishment. So they blame Millard for everything Bainbridge did, and for tempting Bainbridge in the first place. They were quite rough with him when they arrested him. You know how on television they always put a hand on a perpetrator's head when they're helping him get into the backseat of the squad car?"

"So that he won't bump his head."

"Well, this police detective put his hand on Millard's head," she said, "and then slammed it into the roof."

"I've often wondered if that ever happens."

"I saw it happen, Martin. The policeman said he was sorry."

"It must have been an accident."

"Then he did it again."

"Oh."

"I wish I had a tape of it," she said. "I'd watch it over and over."

The woman had heart, Ehrengraf marveled. Her beauty was exceptional, but ultimately it was merely a component of a truly remarkable spirit. He could think of things to say, but he was content for now to leave them unsaid, content merely to bask in the glow of her presence.

And Alicia seemed comfortable with the silence. Their eyes met, and it seemed to Ehrengraf that their breathing took on the same cadence, deepening their wordless intimacy.

"You don't want more coffee," he said at length.

She shook her head.

"The last time you were here—"

"You gave me a Drambuie."

"Would you like one now?"

"Not just now. Do you know what I almost suggested last time?"

He did not.

"It was after you'd brought me the Drambuie, but before I'd tasted it. The thought came to me that we should go to your bedroom and make love, and afterward we could drink the Drambuie."

"But you didn't."

"No. I knew you wanted me, I could tell by the way you looked at me."

"I didn't mean to stare."

"I didn't find it objectionable, Martin. It wasn't a coarse or lecherous look. It was admiring. I found it exciting."

"I see."

"Add in the fact that you're a very attractive man, Martin, and one in whose presence I feel safe and secure, and, well, I found myself overcome by a very strong desire to go to bed with you."

"My dear lady."

"But the timing was wrong," she said. "And how would you take it? Might it seem like a harlot's trick to bind you more strongly to my service? So the moment came and went, and we drained our little snifters of Drambuie, and I went home to Nottingham Terrace."

Ehrengraf waited.

"Now everything's resolved," she said. "I wanted to give you the check first thing, so that would be out of the way. And we've said what we needed to say about my awful husband and that wretched policeman. And I find I want you more than ever. And you still want me, don't you, Martin?"

"More than ever."

"Afterward," she said, "we'll have the Drambuie."

THE BUBBLE MAN OF ALLENTOWN

BY DIMITRI ANASTASOPOULOS
Black Rock

The Bubble Man sat by his open window on the fourth floor of a town house on the corner of Allen and Elmwood. As he settled an aluminum hoop the size of a Frisbee into a tray of soapy water with one hand, he drank from a cup of lemonade with the other, then lifted the hoop in front of a fan. Bubbles floated onto the street below, much to the delight of passersby and children. Day after day he sat by his window blowing bubbles, as soap water bleached the pine floor beneath his flip-flops.

Across the street, Andre Tippett sipped green tea at a café. He had spent the afternoon in a haze, just watching the bubbles. Nowhere to go, nothing to do. A couple weeks ago, he'd been suspended from his work as a crime scene investigator for the county sheriff's office, thanks to a prank he had played with some neighborhood kids. He chose not to fight his suspension. Instead he whiled away the days and waited.

Setting down his cup, he looked up at the fourth-floor window. He had lived in the neighborhood for a little more than nine years, and the Bubble Man had been at it since at least the time Tippett had arrived. He thought of the Bubble Man as a presence who gave Allentown its vibe. Whatever happened in the neighborhood, the Bubble Man was always there.

Although he liked the idea of the Bubble Man, Tippett was also wary. Once he even searched for him on the sex offender registries. Any man who spends his entire day blowing bubbles into the street is an object of deep and abiding suspicion.

This was the second face of Buffalo, the envious one, the paranoid profile, the side opposite the one everyone liked to project. Opposite the civil and the polite, the one that buried secrets and reveled in the misery of others. The one that waited for the Bubble Man to transgress.

Earlier that week, two Buffalo police detectives from the Delaware substation had canvassed the streets after the disappearance of a neighborhood woman, Lora Gastineau. Tippett knew both detectives personally from crime scenes. Gastineau had last been seen walking to a hardware store on Allen, wearing only a slip and sneakers. She told her husband that she'd only be gone a minute, but she never returned. The two detectives knocked on Tippett's door, and when he opened it, they looked past him into his living room and beyond to the kitchen. They were all business, even with colleagues, Tippett thought. When they were on a case, they treated that person as though he had something to hide, even Tippett. Their gaze was bearable only if regarded from a distance, as in a court of law, or else while standing in line at the bank, or picking lettuce out at the grocery.

Of course, they had come to Tippett's door specifically looking for his housemate Steve. Tall Steve with the bleached mohawk, Steve who returned home from the bars each evening and cackled his trademark "Holy hell!" as he slammed the front door, Steve who called in falsetto—"Anybody home?"—as he plodded up the stairs, stumbling two-thirds of the way up before finding his bed and collapsing onto the mattress. The detectives had come because of Steve's prior history: three years ago he'd been charged with kidnapping an underage girl to a Fort Erie casino. Steve and the girl had stayed in Canada overnight, and the girl, to save herself from her parent's anger, swore she had been forced to go. Eventually she revealed that on prior occasions—though not this time because Steve had been so drunk—they had sex.

Eighteen at the time to the girl's sixteen years of age, Steve spent half a year in lockup for statutory rape (the kidnapping charge was dropped). That's where Tippett got to know him. The county sheriff's prison cells were in the same wing as the county forensics lab, and Tippett occasionally encountered Steve in the prison library (a security breach, to say the least), where they discussed their love for old underground comic books. The talks never revolved around plots or characters but rather around R. Crumb vs. S. Clay Wilson, or the influence of Spain Rodriguez. Though Tippett was in his midsixties and Steve in his early twenties, they became fast friends, and after Steve's release, he moved to Tippett's apartment where he read comics for much of the day and drank beer, while waiting to hear back about jobs he'd eventually get fired from.

Tippett yelled for his housemate to show his face. Though it was only noon, Steve shuffled down the stairs drunkenly, shirt full of bloodstains. "Oh God," Tippett moaned. And with that, the detectives took Steve to their precinct and began pumping him with questions.

"Tell us about Lora Gastineau." But Steve said he knew nothing about the woman. He swore that the blood on his shirt was from a fracas at Fisty's Saloon. The detectives didn't buy it. Fisty Carroll, the one-armed owner, a man of ill repute, had apparently and very suddenly attacked Tommy Callahan, the catcher for Buffalo's Triple-A baseball team. According to Steve, Callahan had been sitting at a table along with two girlfriends, one of whom invited Steve to sit with them for a drink. Everything was fine, and then in the middle of a sentence, Callahan tipped right over in his seat and passed out, spilling beer everywhere. It was eleven in the morning, and he was very drunk. The mess had sent the usually calm Fisty over the top. He grabbed hold of Callahan's neck and tried to chew off the man's ear. He bit it, pulling so forcefully that the catcher's ear stretched like rubber, until the eardrum burst, then disintegrated altogether as though Fisty had sucked it out of the canal.

Steve's story amused the two detectives. They were responsible enough, however, to at least check it out with the officers in uniform down the hall. After three hours of interrogation, they received word: Officer Blackmon verified Steve's story. Every detail was true. Fisty was already out on bail after appearing before Judge Adams. And with the awareness that a colorful bar fight out of an old Hollywood wrestling film really did take place in the city of Buffalo—a scene replete with violence, descriptive nicknames, and even war wounds—the detectives released Steve, who didn't waste the afternoon. He walked right back to Fisty's.

When Steve later recounted the whole story, Tippett fixed on one detail that had been contested—whether or not Fisty had sucked out Callahan's eardrum. As baseball fans later found out, the drum had in fact disappeared and Callahan's catching career suffered: he couldn't hear the umpire call balls and strikes, and he often lost balance, keeling over backward when he squatted behind the plate. All that was left in his canal was a knot of withering nerves exposed to the whistling wind.

A week after Lora Gastineau's disappearance, Tippett agreed to meet the detectives at Betty's on Virginia Street. From the outdoor table where they sat, they viewed the backside of buildings on Elmwood. Many were in bad shape. Dark ivy-covered walls, broken roofs. Above the buildings in the distance loomed Bass Pro Tower, one of the city's few skyscrapers, now abandoned. A brown hulk erected in the 1970s, it broke with the city's boldly elegant turn-of-the-twentieth-century facades, its dark tinted windows concealing its empty floors.

Tippett hardly touched his coffee: he'd only ordered one because he wanted the detectives to know Steve had nothing to hide, that though Steve excelled at finding trouble, he was actually a good kid.

Barry, the shorter of the two, shuffled in his seat, as Maurice reached down into his briefcase, gently laid a pen on the table with the other hand, then abruptly pulled out a plain blue notebook with a picture of Gastineau paperclipped to the cover. Tippett recognized her from the news, but he had rarely seen her around the neighborhood. She was married to an optometrist who practiced downtown. Tippett struggled to imagine how Steve might have known her.

She looked very young in the photograph, maybe twenty-five. Why were the detectives using an old photo? The woman was at least forty.

As they ran through the case, the detectives explained what they had learned so far. They then described some of the sketchier characters around Allentown, asking Tippett if he had anything to add.

"Maybe she'll come back," Tippett said. "Maybe she's bored."

A long silence. Barry twirled his pen around his fingers like a baton. "You know about the others," he said. "The ones that haven't been publicized." He asked Tippett about the last time he'd seen Ms. Gastineau, and whether he'd ever seen her with Steve.

Tippett hadn't been hiding anything. But he remembered seeing the optometrist awhile back through the big street-level glass windows of Cantina Loco. Mr. Gastineau had been talking to a young girl at the bar, and Tippett noted it. "Harmless flirting," he said. "Maybe his wife didn't mind."

Tippett was speculating—he knew practically nothing about the couple. The two detectives didn't say anything.

On the next Monday night, Tippett received a call from Gary Yepremian who told him that a body had been discovered in Black Rock. This was the first call from his boss in a couple weeks: Tippett, it seemed, was back on the job. Time to prove himself. In minutes, he made it to Black Rock and found the building, an auto collision shop a stone's throw away from the International Railway Bridge. Since the area was surrounded by barbed-wire fence, he needed to cross over the canal in back of the shack in order to access the body. He thought nothing of commandeering one of the skiffs he found beached on a bike path below the Niagara Thruway; he paddled across the canal to a little ramshackle house crumbling on a tiny beach next to the auto collision shop. Bottles floated by, dead fish, broken planks, tree limbs. His boss had said that the corpse had already been identified as Dora Sanford, wife of Lucky, who had recently opened a new business in Black Rock. They had a child last year.

While paddling, Tippett thought of the day when Yepremian suspended him for coloring in an outline of a county councilman's run-over mastiff as children from the neighborhood gathered around. One told Tippett that he hoped to become a crime scene investigator himself. None of them, however, had seen the car that hit the dog. It was a cloudless day. And the children cajoled Tippett until he removed a chalk stick from his bag and began to color in the mastiff's outline, making a real show of his skills. He was simply humoring them—he knew a good forensic scientist should never draw an outline, as it contaminates the crime scene. When Councilman Bert Jones arrived, he was angry, not only that his dog had been killed, but that the artistic representation of its death had brought cheer to others.

Crossing the canal, Tippett was glad for another chance to collect evidence. A few decades ago, he'd been trained to draw outlines when a body had to be moved quickly. But crime scene procedures had changed over the years. For instance, his colleagues began to use miniature triangle placards numbered according to body parts instead. This was common practice for a few years until Tippett pointed out to his bosses that the triangles were reused at other crime scenes, thereby contaminating blood samples from one scene to the next. After that, the investigators used index cards, which they disposed of afterward. Occasionally, when no one else was around, Tippett broke out his chalk and drew for old time's sake. He'd later blame his chalk outlines on rookie cops who arrived at the scene prior to him. "Chalk Fairies," he called them: they'd draw and disappear. Secretly, he took special pride in etching the most telling lines around a body. In the early 1970s his lines were severe and exact, the best around. He accounted for even the slightest fold in a pant leg, a skill appreciated especially by the families of the deceased who scrutinized photographs of Tippett's outlines for a hint of their loved one's final moments. They recomposed and reenacted entire scenes from an outline of parted lips and heaving tongue that may have formed, Tippett liked to think, the shape of dying words.

He climbed off the boat and began walking up a set of rickety wooden steps to a landing where he would find the body. It was dark but the lights of the thruway on the other side of the canal shone brightly. When he got to the landing, there was no sign of the body. Which sometimes happens. Maybe a crank call. He was about to walk back down to the rocky beach when he noticed, as he looked down, a chalk outline. He stopped, walked around the sketch, studied the figure until, at last, he was satisfied that the outline was of a human body.

Strange. His work had already been done. But by who? He bent to study it: two amateurish semicircles at midleg, possibly the kneecaps. The concave areas were more impressive. The armpits, the throat, the groin each displayed an eye for retrospective invaginations. In those areas, Tippett had to admit, the lines were fine. The artist drew okay, even if he needed to improve his straights, adjust his wrist parallel to the ground when drawing a leg, since his lines were blurry there.

As Tippett walked around the sketch, he stepped on something soft and crunchy, a Ziploc sandwich bag. Inside it: a nose and two fingers. The nose had a large bump. Tippett looked at the sketch and noticed that the mystery artist had outlined a bump as large as the one on the nose in the plastic bag. The hands had been tucked under the outline, however, so it was impossible to tell if they'd been drawn with or without the missing fingers. Tippett wondered: had the outline been drawn before the nose and fingers were severed? Or had the artist taken a postmortem liberty?

The artist had tinkered with the body's appearance after the person had died, Tippett guessed—a new-age sketch artist, judging by the aura of the total work on the ground. It betrayed the artist's faith in symmetry and harmony, in the reconstruction of the whole figure. Techniques popularized in the early 1980s, Tippett thought. By comparison, Tippett was an expert in postwar methods, and operated on the principle that the outline of every dead body had to be drawn exactly. You shouldn't unduly distort proportions by emphasizing a body's innocence.

He knew what he had to do next. He had to secure the crime scene, make sure no one tampered with anything else. He telephoned to see what was taking the detectives so long. An hour passed. To keep dry, he climbed up onto a porch and huddled there, shivering. Soon, he fell asleep.

When he awoke a thick fog had rolled in and he was alarmed to see that the water had risen a foot. It now covered the outline of Dora Sanford. In fact, there was nothing left of her. He heard the water lapping the building—and, faintly, from somewhere below the porch, the sound of someone breathing.

"Hello?" he whispered. No one responded. Finally, he peered down. The thruway lights caught someone's breath rising as mist directly below him.

Tippett slowly walked down the porch stairs and, landing with a splash, began to slog his way to the other side of the concrete base. The breathing became louder. Biting his lip, he sloshed another inch closer, peered around a corner. He saw a large muscled man, his jumpsuit reading *Auto Collisions* on the back, his name, *Lucky*, embroidered on the front pocket. With one arm, the man held a woman's body to his chest, kept her head above the water as he performed mouth-to-mouth resuscitation. The woman's face had no nose. The man, however, had silver pork-chop sideburns, a dimple that seemed to pierce straight through his cheek. His ears had shriveled like dry jellyfish in the cold. Whereas the woman in his arms looked bloated. Her translucent skin covered her bones in a porcelain sheen made even paler by the fluorescent streetlights.

As of yet, the man hadn't noticed Tippett. He was too busy puffing mouth, pumping chest.

Eventually, Tippett moved beside him. The man looked up. His eyes trailed off to the black bag Tippett held in his hand.

"Doctor?"

"No," Tippett hesitated.

The man stared and then tilted his head. He went back to what he had been doing: pumping her chest with his hands, heaving again as her throat gurgled and water spilled from her mouth. He kept puffing anyway. Tears were streaking down his cheeks; wisps of hair stuck to his face with every pump.

Tippett shook him lightly by the shoulder, but he wouldn't separate from the woman's purple lips. He pleaded but the man did not budge. In order to lead him gently from his shock, Tippett decided to play along, and so he covered the cavity where the woman's nose once was. Beneath his fingers, her raw flesh was frozen. Still, he tried pressing hard to force the air back in. He pressed his palms down and was able to hold on just long enough to help the man send some air to her lungs.

The man sat there a few more seconds. He had to know by now that hopes of resuscitating her were wasted. Suddenly, he stood up; then began dragging her body away through the water. At first, Tippett sat dumbfounded as he watched the man lift her into the skiff, and when he understood the man was about to leave him stranded there, his heartbeat quickened. Never before had Tippett witnessed a crime taking place. He much preferred the role of a straggling investigator, always arriving after the fact, in time only to reconstruct a scene, label the evidence, compose a portrait that stayed still long enough for a complete investigation. In his field, there was no call for works-in-progress.

He scuttled over to the man and grasped hold of his jumpsuit sleeve, but the man pushed him down, untethered Tippett's borrowed skiff, then paddled away with the corpse of Dora Sanford, leaving Tippett stranded on the beach.

After climbing back up to the dry porch, his clothes soaking, he sat waiting for the detectives who finally arrived an hour later. Tippett said nothing about what he had witnessed, and five minutes after they rescued him, they all departed the scene.

Tippett arrived home well after the morning commute. The door to his apartment had been left unlocked, which was no surprise given his roommate's recent state of mind. When he walked in, he saw Steve's undershirt tossed under the kitchen table, and a half-filled glass of orange juice (likely a vodka screwdriver) sat next to a spread-out newspaper. Tippett could barely muster up a sufficient amount of disgust at the sight of it; he was still thinking of the previous night's events. Again and again, he searched the auto collision shack of his mind for an explanation of what had happened. That's what bugged him now, not Steve sleeping off another hangover upstairs. In fact, Tippett was so disturbed by the man who hauled off Sanford's body that it took him awhile to notice the newspaper on the table, and the red circle drawn around a picture of Lora Gastineau on the front page.

Steve hadn't stirred the entire time, and though Tippett had half a mind to wake him up so his roommate could accompany him to the café, he decided against it. He'd rather sit alone today as the evening arrived. And besides, Steve's charm, that puerile innocence that transports men (mainly men) of all ages back to boyhood, had worn off, and now Steve was as irritable and resentful as the fan-letter critics published on the back pages of Tippett's favorite comic books. The men had bonded over the idea that there was truth, valor, and heroism in the world: that's what they'd discussed in the prison library. But during the days that Steve trolled the Allentown bars for free drinks and Tippett stiffly ignored the gruesome violence that confronted him on his job, they remained oblivious to the many ways that life, like art, and even like some comic books, had deflowered them. Steve had always liked the comic book villains as much as the heroes. In detention, he understood very well the balance between them. But on the streets of Buffalo, he began to appreciate the darker side, like Spain's nefarious JFK, and though he'd never quite tamp down his love for an avenging Joan Dark, he began to think of Spain's Che as just superficially good, not truly good. He despised such smarmy deifications. Steve had changed. His Buffalo had changed. Life was more about corruption and lies, an aesthetic that the best comic authors would admit into their pristine universe. If art could be moral and full of valor, it could also be perverse, debauched, and destructive, in the best ways possible. Even the sketch of a corpse's outline, though revealing the artist's sensibility, roots into abundant misery. You can enjoy a sketch of a corpse, if you ignore the violence and brutality that preceded it.

Sitting outside the café at a small table, Tippett determined not to let his optimistic disposition sink him. It wouldn't get the best of him, he thought. He shut his eyes, inhaled his mint tea, and sipped. When he opened his eyes, he looked across the street at the CowPök Tattoo gallery and admired the sign above the entrance. An umlaut, very clever. Two of the tattoo artists sat on a sofa opposite the door, hands folded behind their heads, their accustomed pose. Tippett saw them clearly through the plate glass—nothing obstructed his view today nor distracted him. He hadn't noticed yet, but there were no soap bubbles floating down upon the intersection of Allen and Elmwood. No bubbles to comfort Tippett and assure the neighborhood that there are people in this world with habits that die hard. For at least nine years, bubbles had rained down on this intersection every single day. Bubbles that, however familiar and steady, invariably filled you with joy. Many times before, Tippett had thought how heroic it was to blow bubbles day after day, with a doggedness that insisted people were more than outlines one glimpsed through plate-glass windows, a steely will that pushed through the boredom of sitting by a fan day after day, waving one's hoop, a will that mocked the old ego that wailed and gnashed its teeth and insisted there were better things to do in this world and better places to be. But today Tippett was not his usual self. As he drank his mint tea, he didn't feel the need to contemplate his surroundings and make of them something more glorious, to color this corner of Buffalo with a dignity beyond its rust-belt reality. No need either to look up at the Bubble Man's fourth-floor window and suspect that anything was amiss, no need to wonder why the top of the Bubble Man's head was visible on his windowsill, why the Bubble Man's face lay in his tray of red soapy water.

Behind the Bubble Man stood a tall dark shape with hair spiked high in a ten-inch mohawk.

PART II

Hearts & Minds

FALLING ON ICE

BY LISSA MARIE REDMOND

South Buffalo

T he wind blowing off the lake stabbed Mike Sullivan's cheeks as he made his way along Downing Street. He pulled the collar of his Carhartt higher. December in Buffalo. It wouldn't have been so bad if he hadn't lost his license three months before. At least tonight he'd been able to stop into Malloy's for a shot after his shift at the cheese factory. One shot led to two, which led to three and now here he was, carless, no girlfriend, shambling drunk down the snow-clogged streets smelling like cheddar.

It was late when he got to his house. The front walk wasn't shoveled and there were no footprints up the driveway. Erin must still be out, he thought as he turned his key in the side door lock. He would yell at his little sister for breaking curfew when she came in and she'd yell back that he wasn't her father. Then she'd stomp upstairs and slam her door.

Mike looked out to see if Erin was with her friends in the church parking lot. Their house butted right up against St. Martin of Tours' property. The neighborhood kids liked to hang out at night and smoke cigarettes in the dimly lit lot. But it was too cold and snowy tonight. The lot was empty.

Mike shook his head and went over to the kitchen table to look for a note. The stove clock said twelve thirty. He pondered whether to call his mom at the hospital. Maybe Erin had gone on a sleepover? Usually his mom would call him on his cell to let him know.

Headlights cast a glow through his kitchen window. A couple of driveways down, a car door slammed. Mike jammed his phone in his pocket, ready to give Erin hell.

A noise in the front hall. Mike craned his head to see the doorknob twisting back and forth. No one used the front door. He went over and turned the dead bolt and threw open the door.

Erin stood on the stoop, face white. She opened her mouth as if to speak, then her eyes rolled back in her head and she pitched forward. Mike barely managed to catch her. Awkwardly, he sank to the hardwood floor, his sister's body limp in his arms. A bubbling sound came from deep in her chest. Despite the snow clinging to her coat, her back felt warm and sticky.

When he took his hand away, it was covered in blood.

An hour later Mike was sitting with his mother in the trauma unit waiting room at Mercy Hospital. Tears ran down both cheeks but she cried silently, clutching Mike's hand in hers. She was still in her scrubs. She'd been on the maternity floor bringing babies into the world when another nurse came in and got her.

His mother's voice brought him back to the present: "Did she say anything? Anything?"

"No, Ma, I already said. She just collapsed. Then I noticed the blood and I could see where it was coming from. I yanked up her coat and she had a big bruise on her back."

"A big bruise," his mother repeated to herself, trying to make sense of it.

There was a knock at the door. They looked up to a doctor in green scrubs standing in the doorway. "Marge? Can I come in?"

Mike's mom jumped up. "Frank, how is she?"

The older man walked in and shut the door behind him. He was carrying all kinds of paperwork under one of his arms. There were no other families in the trauma room that night. Just what was left of the Sullivans.

"She's awake. She's going to be okay, Marge, but we'll have to operate and soon."

"Operate?" Margaret echoed. "Did she say what happened?"

"Her lung is punctured," the doctor went on as if she hadn't spoken. "We need your permission to operate."

"Punctured by what? What's going on?" She had stepped up to Frank, all five-foot-two of her, facing down this doctor she'd worked with for twenty years.

He pulled an X-ray from one of the folders under his arm. Mike's mom snatched it and held it up to the light. "What is that?" she whispered.

"My best guess? Something metal and sharp that pierced her back. To me it looks like the tip of an ice pick."

Mike was now standing next to his mom, looking at the X-ray of his sister's back which clearly showed a long, pointed shaft lodged like a skewer in a side of beef.

"We won't know for sure until we take it out." The doctor reached for the X-ray and slipped it back into its folder. "The surgeon's on his way. Thankfully, the damage could have been a lot worse. If we get in now she's going to be fine, Marge. Come on with me and we'll get all the papers signed." He slipped an arm around her shoulder and started to lead her out of the room.

"Wait!" Mike called. "Did she say anything? Did she say how it happened?"

The doctor reached back under his arm and handed Mike a yellow legal pad. As they left the room Mike stood staring down at the shaky words scrawled across the front of the pad: *I fell on the ice.*

Erin spent six hours in surgery while Mike and his mom dozed on and off in the nurses' lounge. Word of what happened to Erin had swept out of the hospital and across the neighborhood. A steady trickle of people had pooled together in the downstairs waiting room. By nine o'clock over thirty people had crowded in, including five guys from Sully's firehouse. Everyone was milling around with their cups of coffee, whispering about the tragedies the poor Sullivan family had to endure, ready to help out with whatever was needed.

As Mike slept with his coat still on, his mind replayed the last three months of his life like some old tragic black-and-white movie he was the star of. In his hazy brain he saw his mom's cousin Jimmy sitting him down in his pickup truck after liberating Mike from the police station, blood still oozing from a cut on his forehead. He stunk like booze and piss. Jimmy slid into the driver's side, took a good look at Mike, and punched him square in the jaw.

"If your father could see you now," he spat as Mike held his face. "I get you're all fucked up about Afghanistan. I get you're traumatized about losing your dad. You got every excuse there is. But you are twenty-five years old now, almost twenty-six. I can't keep bailing you out. You got a responsibility to your mom and sister." Jimmy ran his hand through his salt-and-pepper hair. They were the thick, callused hands of an ironworker. Someone who had no sympathy for people who weren't willing to work as hard as he did.

"It was an accident." The words were slurred and shaky. "I didn't do this on purpose. I'm sorry," Mike muttered.

"Yeah, well," Jimmy threw the truck into drive, "I was sorry when your dad got crushed in that building and that didn't count for shit either."

Mike's dad had been a Buffalo firefighter. Sully. Everyone looked up to Sully, literally. At almost six-foot-five he was broad-shouldered with a thick, dark handlebar mustache. He had a happy, booming voice that carried through the firehouse and a reputation for taking you places in a burning building no other firefighter could go. He was South Buffalo Irish through and through.

When Mike was sixteen, a junior at Bishop Timon, a chimney had collapsed on Sully. It killed him instantly.

* * *

It's always a big deal when a firefighter dies on duty, especially in South Buffalo where police and fire jobs span generations. But young Mike wasn't prepared for the spectacle. The funeral was televised, cameramen lined each side of the overcrowded church. Mike was up front, flanked by politicians who all got the chance to talk about the tragedy. Firefighters from all over came to the Mass and fire trucks lined the streets as they made their way to the cemetery. Mike stared out the window of the limo at the sea of faces. He felt nothing.

Sully died a hero, of that there was no doubt. And hollowed-out, washed-out Mike was now the head of the house.

Only that didn't work out so well.

When Mike was nineteen and got caught in his second stolen car, it was Jimmy who drove him down to the army recruiters and stood next to him as he signed his life away for six years.

He was no standout in the service. He had just wanted to come home, find a nice girl, or a not-so-nice one, get his union card, and wait for the firefighters' exam. Instead he returned to Buffalo and went out drinking.

One day, everyone in Malloy's was talking about a girl's body the police found in the Tifft Farms Nature Preserve. It had turned out to be Amy Dunston, Mike's date for junior prom.

He hadn't seen Amy in six years but still remembered how pretty she'd been in her pink dress with her red curls pulled up on her head. They'd kissed outside her house for hours, crushing the roses pinned to her gown. He had touched her face, running his thumb over the freckles across her nose. Amy was the prettiest girl he'd ever seen and when he finally walked her to the door, he had knots in his stomach. He wanted to see her again, wanted to see her all summer long.

Three days later, a half ton of bricks crushed his father. Mike never spoke to Amy again, not even when he saw her at the funeral. Life had suddenly become divided into Before and After.

She was from Before, when his life was good. His life After was something else. Some kind of pain that she didn't fit into.

And now this. The police had found her stabbed to death, her long red curls hacked off and her body dumped. He remembered touching that hair, the way it smelled like strawberries, felt like silk.

How something like that could happen in South Buffalo was a mystery. The neighborhood was still strong, unlike other parts of the city that had declined since the steel plants closed. There was very little real crime there. It was still an Irish Catholic enclave that ran on the parish system. Kids still walked to their parish schools in their plaid uniforms. It was a throwback to simpler times. It had its domestics and bar fights, but homicide? That was a shock to the system.

So Michael Sullivan had done the South Buffalo Irish Catholic thing to do: he drank Jameson until he couldn't see straight and drove into a house.

A door slam jolted him awake.

Hospital room. The doctor came in to tell Mike and his mother that the surgery had gone well, Erin was in the recovery room, and a Detective Flannery was there to see them.

Patrick Flannery was well known to Mike and Margaret Sullivan. Not only had he been friends with Sully, he'd gone to grammar school with Marge and lived just two streets over.

Flannery was short and stocky with thick flaming-red hair that stuck up at all angles, framing his round face. He wore a rumpled gray suit jacket under his heavy wool overcoat. In his left hand was a plastic bag, sealed with red evidence tape.

"Marge, Michael. How you two holding up?"

"What happened to my baby?"

He shook his head. "She's still sedated. All we know is she came home with this lodged in her back."

He held up the bag. A rusty metal shiv, five inches long, rested on the bottom.

Marge reached out and touched it through the plastic.

"It's the shaft of an old-fashioned ice pick," Flannery explained. "The kind with the wooden handle that our parents used when we were kids."

"More like the kind our grandparents used."

"How did that get stuck in my sister's back?" Mike demanded.

Flannery turned toward him. "Do you have the paper she wrote on?"

Mike knew the detective regarded him as a failure. He and Jimmy had spent the better part of three years fishing him out of his messes, with no gratitude on Mike's part. Three months ago, when Mike got his last DWI, Flannery told him not to call him anymore until he cleaned up his act.

Mike handed over the yellow legal pad.

"Did she say anything else?"

"No," Mike said. "I don't think she could."

"You called 911 right away?"

Mike fished his phone out of his pocket. "I called 911 at 12:34 a.m." He held the screen out for Pat.

"Notice anything unusual before she came in? Or after?"

"I heard a car pull up, but not in front of the house. A few doors down. Then she was fumbling with the doorknob, like she didn't remember she had a key."

The detective nodded. "She was probably in shock. You never got a look at the car?"

"No. I only saw the headlights and heard the door."

Flannery pulled a notebook out of his coat and jotted down a few things. "Okay, Mike. Come down to the station house, make a statement. Not today. Be here with your mother. But tomorrow for sure. Call my cell when you need a ride. You still got my number?"

Mike tried to keep his voice even. "I know it by heart."

"Good." Flannery gave Marge a long hug.

"Do you think someone did this to her?" Marge asked, pulling away.

"It's possible someone dropped it or meant to throw it out and it froze in the ice. Then she came along and fell on it just right. But I'd like to know where the wood handle is. I don't think she could have walked very far with this thing stuck in her. I checked your yard and around your house. No blood."

"She was wearing a heavy coat," Mike offered.

"I'll stop by your place and grab that."

"It's still on the front hall floor." Mike detached his house key from his ring and handed it to Pat.

"I'll get the photographer and evidence in with me to document the scene while I'm there. I'll leave the key when I'm done."

Mike said nothing.

Marge leaned forward and kissed his cheek. "Thank you, Pat. For everything."

"You just get Erin better." Flannery gave a nod and left.

Mike stayed in the nurses' lounge. He knew the word must be out that he was in the bar drinking whiskey right before Erin got hurt. The latest in his list of fuck-ups. Drunk again when his sister needed him.

He stretched back out on the floral couch. It was about six inches too short to accommodate his long frame. His work boots hung over the side and he still smelled like cheese. If Sully could see his son now. Useless. A disgrace.

In the midst of his self-pity, a thought kept forming at the back of his head. Something about last night. He wished he had a shot to steady himself. In the army he'd stuck to beer, a lot of it, but back at home in the Irish heritage district of Buffalo he'd reunited with his old friend whiskey. It made the cheese smell better.

He patted his flannel shirt until he came up with his pack of smokes. He knew smoking was off-limits in the hospital, but he couldn't hold out any longer. He lit up and eased his head into the cushions. It had been cold yesterday. Erin had told him before he left for work that she was going to Casey's house to watch movies. Casey Keane lived on Red Jacket, close to the hospital. Erin had gone around four, when it was still light out. He'd left a few minutes later, to work a half shift from five until eleven. She should have been home when he got there. Casey's mom would never have let her walk home alone in the dark, but he felt sure that it was not Mrs. Keane who dropped his sister off.

He got up, pulling his coat on. His sister's blood had stained the front.

Casey's house was only a two-minute walk from the intersection of Abbott and Red Jacket. The snow and the wind had picked up since last night, obscuring the sun. It was now ten a.m. and the bluehairs were driving slowly past him on their way to Mass. He picked his way across the icy sidewalks, dangerous enough to fall on. Throw an ice pick into the mix and things could definitely get deadly.

Casey Keane lived in a huge green-and-white double right on the corner. Her grandmother lived in the upstairs flat and Casey's family occupied the lower one. Casey's older brother Wayne was shoveling the driveway when Mike walked up. Wayne was trying to get it down to the pavement, losing the battle with each flake of snow that fell.

Mike stepped up and they shook hands. Wayne looked surprised to see him. He'd been a year behind Mike at Bishop Timon.

"Sorry to hear about your sister. Do they know what happened?"

"Not yet. Doctors say she's doing good, though. Is Casey home?"

"Yeah, she's with my mom. She's all upset."

Mike went to the side door and rang the bell. It occurred to him that no one used the front door in South Buffalo. Always the side.

Casey's mom greeted him. He knocked his work boots

against the door frame and stepped into the side hall. He told her what the doctors said but didn't mention the spike.

Mrs. Keane was built like his own mother, sturdy with graying brown hair and a smattering of tan freckles across her nose. "I asked Casey if anything was wrong when they left Bridget's last night and she said everything seemed fine."

"Bridget?"

"Bridget. They went over her house to watch movies."

Mike nodded. It was odd. Bill Donavan had been at Malloy's last night bragging that his wife and Bridget were in Pittsburgh visiting her brother and he had free rein to enjoy the holiday spirit. "Can I talk to Casey myself?"

She led him back through the living room, past the bathroom to the back bedrooms, pausing in front of a white door decorated with green shamrocks. "Casey!" she shrieked.

The door cracked open. Casey pulled out her earbuds. "What, Mom?"

"Erin's brother wants to talk to you, sweetie. He says she's going to be all right. I'm headed to the hospital to see Marge. Walk him out when you two are done."

"Okay, Ma."

As soon as Mrs. Keane left, Mike's eyes narrowed on the sixteen-year-old girl in front of him. Casey backed up into her room and Mike followed, closing the door behind him. Tears started welling up in her eyes.

"Where were you last night?" he asked in a low voice.

Casey spotted the bloodstains on the front of his jacket. "We were at Bridget Donavan's house . . ."

"Bullshit. Bridget isn't even in Buffalo."

Tears ran freely down her cheeks. "Please, please don't tell my mom."

"I don't give a shit about your mom. My sister is in the hospital with a hole in her back and I want to know where the hell you two really were last night."

Casey had had a mad crush on Mike when she was younger. She had mooned over his blond hair and grass-green eyes. But his angelic appearance had taken a turn after his nose was broken twice. The chip in his tooth from hitting the house twisted his toothpaste smile into a convict's grin. "Liam Fitzgerald had a party at his apartment last night. We went there."

Liam was twenty-one and had an upper apartment off Seneca Street. It was notorious around the neighborhood for underage drinking and drugs.

"How did you get home?"

"We walked there through the park . . ."

"How did you and Erin get home?" He was now up in her face, his breath reeking of cigarettes washing over her mouth and nose.

"Kyle Cuddihy drove me home around eleven. Erin stayed. She was talking to some guy. She said she had a ride."

He grabbed her shoulders. "Who?"

"I don't know!" she sobbed. "He was older, maybe your age. I never saw him before."

Mike released her. "You left your friend at a drinking party with some fucking stranger?"

"I know. I know." She covered her face with her hands. "I'm sorry."

"Not even I would do that, Casey, and I'm a total fuck-up."

She crumpled onto her bed. Mike's phone vibrated in his back pocket with a text from his mom saying Erin was awake.

"You better tell your mother the truth or Detective Flannery will when he gets here."

"Oh please, Mike, no . . ."

He opened the shamrock door and let it slam behind him.

Wayne must have given up on the driveway because he was nowhere to be found and the driveway looked even worse than before. Mike returned to the hospital. The snow was heavier now. Fat flakes squashed against his face, held for an instant.

* * *

At the ICU, Mike's mom sat slumped in a chair across from Erin's bed. She was still wearing her scrubs. Nurses rushed back and forth between the rooms in time to the sound of alarms going off. Erin's room was quiet by comparison. The nurses all knew Mike and let him pass in silence.

Erin lay on the bed with an oxygen mask covering her mouth and nose. Tubes were sticking out of her arm, hooked up to monitors and IVs. Her eyes were closed, dark lashes feathered against her cheeks. She looked younger than her sixteen years. Her blond hair fanned out around her face, which was so pale it shocked him.

His mother held a finger to her lips and whispered, "She's asleep."

"Did she say anything?"

"It's hard for her to talk. She said she walked home and fell on the ice." She shook her head. "I don't know, Mike. It could have happened. The ice pick could have been frozen upright and she could have fallen on it."

"You believe that?"

"What else could it be? Why would she lie?" Marge had dark circles under both eyes. She sighed and stood up. "I'm going to get a coffee. I want someone to be here when she wakes up again."

"Go ahead, Mom. I got it."

She put a hand against the side of his face and smiled weakly, "You're a good boy, Michael. Even if you don't know it."

As she disappeared down the hall, Mike stood for a minute listening to the heart monitors and breathing machine. Finally he said, "I know you're awake, Erin."

With one hand she held the oxygen mask away from her mouth. "Hi, Mike."

"How do you feel?"

"It hurts to breathe." Now he was over her bed, stroking

her hair. They had the same color eyes, their father's eyes.

"I was just at Casey's," he said gently. "I know about the party."

"Don't tell Mom." It came out raspy, pleading and desperate.

He shook his head. "No promises. Not this time."

"Please, just don't tell her now." She coughed and let the mask fall back on her face. She took some slow, shaky breaths and pulled it back again. "I'll tell you, but don't tell her yet, okay?"

"Okay," he lied.

"There was this older guy at the party. I think his name was Brandon or Brendon. I never saw him before." She stopped and took another couple of pulls off her mask. "He was really nice and really cute. Casey wanted to leave with Kyle, and Brendon said he'd drive me home. I said okay but that I had to get home before you. So we left and got into his car. It was red, a two-door."

She started to cough again and it hurt her. Mike held her hand while she tried to catch her breath. The pain knotted up her face as she breathed in and out, in and out. When she finally managed to get her wind, she went on: "He took me through Cazenovia Park. At first I thought he was just cutting through from Seneca to Abbott Road, but then he started going down all these dark streets. Then he just stops. He says, *Something's wrong with the engine.* And he gets out and pops the hood up. He looks under the hood then calls back to me and tells me to hold it up for him, he needs to get something out of his tool box to fix the car. So I get out and I start holding up the hood, even though it's freezing and snowy. He goes around to the back of the car and gets something out of the trunk. Then all of a sudden he punches me in the back as hard as he can. I was so shocked I dropped the hood and started to run. He came running after me, yelling that he was sorry and didn't know why he did that. I had to stop because I couldn't breathe. He grabbed me and was crying, saying he didn't know why and that he'd drive me home as long as I promised not to tell anyone . . ." She gasped a little, hiccupping as she struggled to talk.

"And it was so cold and I was scared and couldn't breathe so I got back into his car. He drove me home and cried the whole way, reminding me I promised not to tell anyone what happened. I was so scared because he knew where I lived. And I couldn't breathe. I didn't know he stuck me with anything. He pulled in front of the Glazers' house and let me out. I don't know how I made it home. I don't remember."

She slipped the mask back over her mouth. The window next to her bed was shaking from the howling wind. Mike glanced up at the television mounted on the wall. A scrolling ticker announced a winter storm warning.

He turned back to his sister. "What did this guy look like?"

"Your age, I guess. Dark hair. Not as tall as you, but tall. He was really good looking and he seemed so . . . so . . . He seemed so nice." The tears came again.

Mike considered her story. Liam Fitzgerald might know who the guy was. But the truth was that his apartment had become a kind of speakeasy for underage girls and potheads. He'd gone there a couple times himself since he'd been home, before he lost his car. The thought of his little sister in a place like that made him want to burn it to the ground.

"The car," Mike said suddenly, latching onto something. "Why did you have to hold the hood open? Why didn't it stay open on its own?"

"It was an old car, from the sixties or whatever. The kind guys like to restore. And it was loud—on-purpose loud, not bad-muffler loud."

That was when it clicked, what he couldn't remember that morning. Mike didn't just see the headlights, he heard the car.

A souped-up car.

A red classic, driven in the Buffalo winter by a guy his age named Brendan or Brandon.

Brandon Gates.

Brandon had been a year behind Mike at Bishop Timon. His nickname had been Movie Star because he was so pretty. He'd been captain of the baseball team and class president, dated the hottest girl at Mount Mercy Academy. He'd strut around the halls, even as a freshman, cocky as hell. He ended up getting a full ride to some big-name college and everyone said he was going to play in the majors. He was going to be the next Warren Spahn. Then something happened his freshman year and he came home. He lived in his mother's house, not far from the Sullivans. No one ever saw him outside. Mike had seen the red car drive by the taverns late at night, cruising the neighborhood. People said he worked on the car all day and only took it out after his mother fell asleep. The neighborhood had all kinds of theories on what had turned him into a hermit. Some said drugs. Some said it was a bad situation with a girl. No one knew for sure.

Mike leaned in and kissed Erin's forehead. "Get some rest."

"What are you going to do?"

"Let you sleep." He settled the oxygen mask on Erin's face and gave her a sad smile. She closed her eyes. "Don't worry about anything."

Mike zipped his jacket up tight and headed for the elevator banks.

Now the winds were so fierce that it was impossible to see three feet ahead. Mike could navigate the South Buffalo streets with his eyes closed, though, and he leaned into the wind, his ears without sensation. To the south the bells of Aquinas were pealing noon. Cars crawled along at five miles an hour. The street signals were nothing but faint red and green frosted ghosts above the invisible road.

By the time he had turned onto Downing from Abbott it was a full-blown snowstorm. Mike walked across the church parking lot and entered his house through the side door. He looked across the kitchen to the front hall. The police had been there. Between them and the ambulance drivers from last night there was all kinds of debris left on the floor mixed in with his sister's blood. He'd clean up that mess later.

In the middle of the kitchen table was his key and a note:

Don't think there's any burglars out today so I left the door open. Don't forget to see me tomorrow.
Pat

Mike crumpled the note and went upstairs, trailing wet bootprints. He stopped in front of his mother's bedroom door, pausing with his hand on the knob. He took a deep breath and walked in.

The room itself was simple. A plain wooden bed frame held a queen-size mattress. The matching dresser sat against the wall with a lace doily draped across it, his mother's perfumes and lipsticks arranged along the top. His grandmother's rocking chair sat in the far corner covered by an ancient quilt. His mother liked to keep everything hospital-neat.

On the far wall was a framed family portrait taken the year before his father died. Mike looked happy and young next to his bear of a father. Sully's massive hand was resting on Mike's shoulder. Erin looked like a mini version of his mom, pixie cut and crooked teeth.

Mike went to his mom's closet, opened the door, and felt around the highest shelf. His fingers managed to grab the edge of a shoe box, which he carefully took down. Inside was his dad's silver revolver. He hadn't held it in a long time. Once when he was seventeen he sat on the bed and held it to his forehead for two hours. He wasn't sure why, what his endgame had been at the time, but now his reason for taking it was crystal clear.

Mike slid the gun into the waistband of his jeans and pulled his flannel shirt over the butt.

He grabbed his black knit hat from his room and tugged it down over his ears. He zipped his coat up and threw himself out into the storm.

Brandon Gates lived on Britt Avenue, almost directly behind the Sullivans. It occurred to Mike that if Brandon looked out one of his second-story windows he could see right into their backyard.

Mike trudged along Downing, cut the corner, and came back up Britt. He could see the outline of the boxy beige house only when he was right on top of it. He vaguely remembered going to a keg party there when he was in high school and stumbling home in the dark. His dad had held onto his shirt as he puked in the backyard, then put him to bed. The next morning Sully had him up at the crack of dawn cleaning out the gutters for punishment.

Mike shook off that memory and scanned the house through the blowing snow. The attached garage door was closed. He could see the flicker of a television through the front window. He walked up to the side door and pounded hard.

After a moment a gray-haired woman wearing a flowered housecoat opened the door. "Yes?" she asked, with a mix of curiosity and politeness.

"Is Brandon home?"

"Are you one of Brandon's friends?" She opened the door wide, inviting him to come in out of the cold. "His friends never come over anymore. Did you go to school with Brandon?"

"Yes ma'am. We went to Bishop Timon together." He stepped further into the red and white kitchen lovingly done up with apple decorations.

"I'm sorry, sweetie, I don't remember you. Early-onset Alzheimer's, they say." She tapped a finger to her forehead. "But I think I'm just getting old."

"Is Brandon home?"

"Mom?"

Mike turned to see Brandon Gates standing in the doorway between the kitchen and the living room. If Mike wasn't in Brandon's own house he would never have recognized him. He was slim but extremely muscular, like he spent his days down in the basement lifting weights. His dark hair, which had always been cut short and neat when he was an athlete, now hung shaggy to his shoulders and was slicked back. He wore a white T-shirt, faded jeans. He looked to Mike like some fifties greaser.

As soon as Brandon realized who was standing in his kitchen, all the color drained from his face. Mike walked forward, pulled the gun from his waistband, and shoved it in his gut. "Brandon, you and me need to go for a ride."

"But my shows are on and I don't know how to change the channel anymore," his mother protested. "You can't leave when my shows are on!"

"Change the channel for your mother," Mike growled, and backed him into the living room.

"Don't do this, man," Brandon whispered as Mike stuck the remote in his hand. "Please, man, this is all a mistake." But Mike pressed the gun harder and Brandon began to flip through the channels.

"I can't leave my mother alone, Mike, you don't understand."

Mike put a hand on Brandon's shoulder and got behind him, the barrel of the gun between his shoulder blades. "You're all set, Mrs. Gates. Me and Brandon are just going to take a little ride."

"But the weather is terrible! And what if the phone rings? Brandon? You can't leave me!" she called out desperately.

"It's okay, Mom. I'll be right back. I promise." He let Mike push him toward the door to the attached garage.

"Brandon? Brandon?" she wailed, as Mike opened the door and prodded Brandon through.

"How come you didn't tell her to call the police? Hmm?" Mike breathed into his ear. "You don't want them to find out what you did?"

"This is all a mistake, okay?"

Mike walked him down the garage stairs. The cherry-red Mustang sat idle among various toolboxes and spare parts. It was obvious he spent a lot of time working on the car, alone in the garage. Mike guessed Brandon pumped iron all morning and then spent the rest of his day replacing spark plugs, changing channels for his mom once in a while.

Mike pushed him to the passenger-side door, ignoring his protests. Even in the dim light he could see a dark stain on the fabric of the passenger seat. On the floor of the driver side was a small wooden handle. It was rounded, like a jump rope grip.

"I didn't mean to hurt your sister! I just wanted to give her a ride home. I saw her and her friend walking through the park and that's not safe . . ."

"So you followed them?"

"I just wanted to help her. I've seen her since she was a little girl!"

Watched her, Mike thought darkly. *You've been watching her.*

"The car was sputtering! I just wanted to check the oil and I slipped. I didn't know I stabbed her, she ran away. When I looked at the handle the tip was gone, I thought it fell out! You have to believe me!"

Mike grabbed onto the collar of Brandon's crisp white tee and rammed his face into the side of the Mustang. "You always check your oil with an ice pick?"

"I just grabbed anything!" he sputtered, blood bubbling up on his lip.

"So why didn't you tell anyone?"

"Because I knew they'd all jump to conclusions. That's why I made her promise not to tell. People always jump to the wrong conclusions!"

Mike pulled him back so he could see Brandon's face. "So this has happened before?"

"Not like this! I never meant to hurt your sister! I didn't mean to kill anyone!"

Mike slammed Brandon's head into the passenger-side window, squashing his nose in a burst of bright red blood. Then a thought raced through his whiskey-enhanced brain. "You didn't kill my sister. She's still alive."

Brandon coughed and spit blood onto the concrete. His greasy hair was falling apart, framing his face in stringy strands.

"You killed Amy Dunston."

As soon as he said it out loud, Mike knew it was a fact. As sure as he plunged an ice pick into Mike's sister's back, Brandon Gates had murdered Amy Dunston.

"You don't understand," Brandon croaked weakly, blood pouring from his broken nose.

"You killed Amy," Mike repeated, and spun Brandon around, shoving the gun up under his chin.

"No, Mike, you gotta believe me. We were friends, right? We used to hang before . . . before—"

"Shut your mouth." Mike pushed him hard against the car frame. With his free hand he fished his cell phone out of his back pocket. He hadn't charged the thing since before he went to work almost twenty-four hours before. It was dead. He threw it down on the floor and grabbed Brandon's collar again.

He needed a phone and a little help.

"Put your boots on. We're going for a walk."

Mike kept the gun trained on the back of Brandon's head as he pulled on a pair of Timberlands. "Can I get my coat?" The blood from his nose had soaked his T-shirt, making an exclamation point on his chest.

"Hell no. It's not far. We're just going up to the church." Mike hit the button on the wall and the garage door rose, exposing them to the storm outside. The church was only half a block up but it was slow going in the blustering wind. Brandon blubbered the whole way.

"This is a misunderstanding! Your sister is alive! She's fine!"

"What about Amy?" Mike snarled, pushing him forward.

"That was a misunderstanding too! I can see, Mike, how you would think what you do, but those were just accidents. Accidents happen."

"Like your nose was an accident?"

His teeth were chattering. "Yes! Yes! Just like that, and I promise I'll never tell anyone you did that, and it will be all right."

"Like you made Erin promise?"

"Yes! Like that! And see, she is fine. She promised not to call the police and she's okay!"

"But Amy didn't promise, did she? And it wasn't okay."

"Amy Dunston was a fucking whore!"

Mike spun him around and hit him in the mouth with the gun. Brandon fell back into a snowdrift at the edge of the parking lot.

It struck Mike as odd at that moment that he could just make out his own house from where he now stood. He grabbed Brandon by the front of his shirt and pulled him out of the snow, leaving a few of his teeth behind.

Mike continued to shove him across the lot to the rear entrance of the church. They had let his family in that way for his father's funeral. Mike managed to get the half-frozen Brandon into the back hall where the offices were located.

Eleven o'clock Mass was long over and Father Flynn came out of one of the back rooms when he heard the commotion. "What the devil is going on, Michael Sullivan?" he demanded.

Mike stealthily put his gun back in his pants, then shoved Brandon down on his knees. "This man stabbed my sister and killed Amy Dunston."

Father Flynn's eyes widened. "How do you know this? What happened to him?"

"Because the fucker just told me," Mike replied, answering both questions at once.

The portly Irish priest bent down to get a better look at Brandon. "Son, is this true?"

Brandon covered his face with his hands and sobbed. "It's true. It's true. But they were accidents. It was a mistake. I didn't mean to kill Amy." Then, like a lightbulb flickering on in a dark room, a thought seemed to take hold in his brain. He jerked his head up. "But if I confess to you, I'm forgiven, right? If you hear my confession then I'm forgiven and everything is fine." He smiled a sick, bloody, gap-toothed smile, "Everything will be okay."

"Let me take you to the bathroom, son, and clean you up." Father Flynn reached down to help him and hissed the words "Call 911" to Mike, nodding toward the church secretary's office.

"I demand you hear my confession immediately," Brandon lisped as the round little priest helped him toward the small bathroom at the end of the hall.

Mike went for the phone. He dialed Patrick Flannery's number. "Pat, it's Mike. I got the guy."

"What guy? Where are you?"

"The guy who stabbed Erin. The guy who killed Amy Dunston. We're at St. Martin's church, in the back by the offices. It's Brandon Gates. He did it."

"Don't you move. I'm coming now from the hospital. And don't do anything stupid."

Too late, thought Mike. As he put the phone back on the hook he heard a loud crash from the hallway. He raced out of the office to find the priest lying flat on his back, half in the bathroom.

"He pushed me down! He ran out the back door!"

Mike hitched his arms under the priests' armpits and hauled him up. "Are you okay, Father?"

"Aren't you going after him?"

Mike shook his head. "In a minute. But could you do me a favor first?"

* * *

Detective Patrick Flannery must have skidded through every red light to get to St. Martin's. He found the blood-spattered Mike and bruised priest waiting in the narthex. "Where is he?" Pat barked.

"I'll take you to him," Mike offered.

The ride to Brandon's house was short compared to the walk. The garage door was still open and Brandon was sitting behind the wheel of the Mustang, furiously scrubbing at the stain on his passenger seat with an old rag.

Pat drew his gun and approached the car. "Drop that, son. Put your hands in the air and don't even think of turning the car on."

He walked around to the driver-side door and yanked it open. He spotted what Mike had seen: the blood, the handle. Brandon sat like a statue with his hands above his head, staring straight ahead. Pat pulled him out roughly and walked him back to his unmarked gray sedan that was blocking the entrance to the garage. Mike could hear him babbling as Pat snapped a pair of cuffs on him.

"Amy led me on. I used to see her working nights at the gas station. She would smile at me. I know she liked me. Then she wouldn't ride in my car. I had to make her. Then she wouldn't promise not to tell. That was all she had to do. So I stabbed her with my Eagle Scout knife. I cut off all her hair, because it was so pretty, and then I put it under my pillow . . ."

Mike slid out of the front passenger seat and Pat threw Brandon in the back of the car.

"I can't listen to him," Mike muttered, and walked deeper into the garage. Pat trailed after him, talking into his hand-held radio, calling for homicide, evidence, and photography to respond to the scene. When he was finished he ducked his head back into his car and talked to Brandon briefly while Mike lit a cigarette. Mike wondered what Brandon's mother was doing and then realized he didn't care.

"He says you have a gun on you," Pat said, clipping his radio back to his belt, coming toward Mike.

Mike lifted up his jacket and shirt and turned around slowly. "No gun. Want to pat me down? Ask his mother if she saw a gun."

"How'd you get him down to the church?"

"I confronted him. He wanted to confess. Ask Father Flynn." Mike bent down, scooped up his dead cell phone, and tucked it away.

Brandon was now howling louder than the wind.

"What happened to his face?" Pat asked.

"It was an accident," Mike said. "He fell on the ice."

Pat stood silently. "You did a good thing today," he said at last. "Your father would be proud."

"I gotta go, Pat." Mike flicked his cigarette butt against the wall and walked toward the street.

"Don't forget to see me tomorrow," Pat called after him. "Get some sleep, Sully."

Mike paused for a second and then disappeared into the storm.

PARKSIDE

BY S.J. ROZAN
North Park

F rankie was watching through the window when the police came to the Wisnewski's. He spent a lot of time at
that window anyway, making scary monster faces and
claws, growling, snarling, pretending he was about to jump
across the air shaft, sometimes pulling his pants down and
mooning until Petey Wisnewski finally had a tantrum. Then
Petey's mom would come wallop him. By that time Frankie was
out of sight, and old lady Wisnewski never knew what set Petey
off.

It wasn't the first time he saw the cops come to the Wisnewski's. The dad was always beating on the mom, and both of them
smacked the kids around, and sometimes the yelling and screaming was so loud the neighbors called the cops. They'd come and
pretend to be reasonable, but you could see from their shoulders
and the way they were kind of twitchy that they were really saying without using words that they'd throw the mom and dad in
jail and take the kids away if they didn't cool it. So the parents
would cool it for a while, and then something would happen, and
everyone was thumping on everyone else again.

Eddie O'Brien said Frankie should let up on Petey. He said
it wasn't Petey's fault that Frankie's mom made him let Petey tag
along wherever he went just because they were some stupid kind
of cousins, and it wasn't Petey's fault anyway that he was only
five. Eddie had like twenty brothers and sisters, or maybe just
ten, but whatever, he didn't give a shit if little kids were climbing all over him all the time. But for Frankie, since his dad left

it was just his mom and him, and his mom worked all day out at Wegmans. He liked to do what he liked to do and it pissed him off to have Petey stuck to him everywhere. And he wasn't so sure it wasn't Petey's fault. Petey had that mean kind of smile, like his dad's, when Frankie told his mom no but his mom said yes and made him go to the Wisnewski's and take Petey some-place. Frankie figured going to school and doing his homework was enough, and his mom should've been happy with that. Eddie didn't even always do that. What Frankie did, him and Eddie and the guys, after school or weekends when there wasn't Little League or Pop Warner, that should've been his business. Shit, he even went to church with her most Sundays, why couldn't she leave him alone after that?

But no. Say, if Frankie wanted to go up to Parkside Candy for some fudge. That was a great expedition. You had to take the bus up Hertel, and once you got up near the Parkside you could jump on the metro for a detour to downtown. In this city the metro was only underground sometimes, and sometimes in a cut like a tunnel with no roof. Frankie's dad said that was Buffalo right there, you think you're in the sunshine but you're still in a hole. But Frankie liked it because you could close your eyes and pretend you were riding a real subway, in New York or Chicago or someplace, not Buffalo, not all shabby old low buildings and broken-up roads, where dads had to leave to go West to find a job and they didn't come back. And the underground part, as long as you were riding down there you could think that when you came up it was going to be new, all honking traffic and skyscrapers and glass.

Frankie ducked back behind the edge of the window as one of the cops came to look out from the Wisnewski's. The cop's face was all serious and Frankie didn't want the guy to see him spying. The cop turned around again to talk to old lady Wis-newski, who was crying.

The cool thing about going up to the Parkside, Frankie

thought, wasn't just the detour metro ride. It was still Buffalo when you came back, but inside the candy store, the wood gleamed and the mirrors were polished and it was quiet, like everything was slower. Like it was a different Buffalo. His mom said that was the old Buffalo, from a long time ago when everyone had a lot of money. Frankie asked if his dad had a lot of money then too, but she said it was much longer ago than that. Frankie wasn't sure what that meant but he loved to go to the Parkside.

Actually, having Petey along was okay for a while. The first time they went there, the lady gave Frankie extra fudge because she said his little brother was so cute, carrying his teddy bear, holding onto Frankie's shirt. Frankie started to scowl and say, *He's not my brother, he's just my stupid cousin, and besides he has snot all over his face*, but Eddie was there that time and poked him in the ribs. Frankie got what Eddie meant—Eddie was smart— and stopped himself just in time, and the lady smiled and slipped them the extra couple of pieces. Him and Eddie even gave Petey some, and they told him he really, *really* had to never tell anyone they came all the way here, because of course it was way past where they were allowed to go without grown-ups.

That first time worked out fine, so a couple more times Frankie told his mom he was going out to play, his mom told him to take Petey to give Petey's mom a break, Frankie said, *Yeah, yeah*, and they hiked it over to the bus stop, Frankie galloping just a little faster than Petey could go and then turning around to yell at the kid to move it.

The fourth time was the trouble. Petey left the damn teddy bear in the store. What a jerk! They had to go back for it, because Petey wouldn't stop howling. Everyone on the bus was staring at them. They got home late, but it still would've been okay except that little baby Petey started crying when he saw his mommy and told her about almost losing the fucking teddy bear.

That night Frankie's mom beat his butt something fierce.

He was grounded, and even though she wasn't home until supertime she knew if he went out because he had to go over every hour and check in with old lady Wisnewski, who if she wasn't a witch sure looked like one and she smelled bad. He thought she might be drunk enough that she wouldn't notice if he checked in or not, but he wasn't sure so he kept doing it.

Still, a couple of those one-hour times, Frankie raced to the bus and the metro and took a short ride anyway. He couldn't go all the way to the Parkside but instead of imagining he was riding under Chicago he pretended he was on a real train, not the metro, on a long trip West to find his dad. Out West they had horses and deserts, and he wasn't sure but he thought it didn't snow. That would be as awesome as skyscrapers.

The only good part was, as long as Frankie was grounded, stupid little Petey was stuck too. His sister and brothers wouldn't take him with them anyplace, which pissed Frankie off because the brat was much more their job than Frankie's.

Eddie said he should just chill and play with his Wii or something until his mom got tired of the whole grounding thing. But Frankie didn't have a Wii. His mom said they couldn't afford it, which Frankie didn't get because it was only a little thing you held in your hand and pointed at the TV, so how much could it cost? But anyway, he didn't have one, so while he was grounded and thinking about Eddie and the guys running and smashing into each other on the football field without him, it was either watch TV, which was pretty stupid, or make Petey cry, which was fun.

Frankie ducked back once more as the cop looked out the Wisnewski's open window again. He was good at ducking back, from all those times old lady Wisnewski came to see what Petey was yowling about before she smacked him. Now she wasn't smacking anybody, just crying, and she didn't say anything when the cop seemed to be asking her why the window was open on a cold day like this. She just kept crying and he shook his head. He was one of the cops who'd come before, and he gave his partner that kind of look that said he knew something like this would happen. They always thought they were so smart, cops. Jerk. He didn't look for a second at the rope that ran between the buildings. Even if he had, he wouldn't have seen anything on it, but if he was so smart he should have looked, and then he should have said, *That's not a clothesline, who'd hang clothes to dry in a stupid dark air shaft like this?*

When the cops left they took old lady Wisnewski with them, and one of Petey's brothers who was home. Frankie couldn't see the door shut but he heard it because the window was open. He realized: now he could go out. What could his mom say? Old lady Wisnewski wasn't there to check in with. He could even say he'd tried, which was going to be a lie, because he was headed out to the football field right now. Well, almost right now. He checked the kitchen clock. He had plenty of time. First he'd go to the bus and then to the metro and ride a few stops, and then, when he was someplace else, he was going to stuff Petey's stupid teddy bear in the metro station garbage pail. That's what Petey had opened the window to try to get, after Frankie had made a noose and hung it from the rope. There it was, dangling, with Frankie putting his hands around his own throat and making a cross-eyed, choking face. Petey had howled and cried, and slammed his fists, and snot ran out of his nose, but Frankie had just laughed and made the choking face again. So Petey opened the window and stood on the sill and reached too far, and then had fallen, which is why the cops came.

Frankie decided he'd better wait to go out until the ambulance guys and cops down there stopped taking photos and measuring things, and finally covered Petey all up and took him out of the courtyard. He'd seen it on TV, that that's how it went with bodies. Then he'd go play football, smash and slam and pound with the other guys. But on the way, after he got rid of the stupid bear, he'd go up to the Parkside. He didn't have much money, but that was okay. The lady there would give him extra fudge for his cute little brother, who couldn't come with him today.

CHICKEN NOODLE'S NIGHT OUT

BY JOHN WRAY & BROOKE COSTELLO

Anchor Bar

I n the faux-Gothic dining hall of my North Buffalo prep school hung a painting of a kid who'd died young. Nobody knew how he'd died, exactly, but his watery eyes and primly parted straw-colored hair didn't speak too highly for his constitution. I always suspected he'd expired from an acute attack of privilege.

It was under this painting, at the end of lunch period on the first day of senior year, that Christian "Chicken Noodle" Potelesse told me the story of his own brush with mortality, in the form of two plus-size women, a stretch Buick LeSabre, and a man by the name of Rick James. Noodle had never talked to me before, not even to tell me to get out of his way; but on that morning—the morning after the Incident—he clutched at my sleeve like a Victorian urchin, pale and bruised and diminished, and held me there until he'd told his tale. It was plain to see that he'd gotten his ass kicked, but that wasn't what gave me the willies: his eyes had a sunken, haunted look to them, as if the person heretofore known as "Christian Potelesse" were no longer in permanent residence. Here's the story, as far as I can recollect it.

Chicken Noodle was sitting in the Anchor Bar, suffering through a date with a girl too smart for him by half, when the door to Main Street blew open and The Man Himself rolled in with his standard entourage: two girls on one arm and his wife on the other. He'd just been released from Folsom Prison (yes, *that* Folsom Prison), but you wouldn't have known it from his Panavision grin. When he came through the door everyone in the place stood up and clapped. It made no difference that James and his brand-new wife, Anne Hijazi, had just done two years for kidnapping, rape, and aggravated assault; Buffalo has ever stayed true to its own.

The girls didn't seem to mind either, as far as Chicken Noodle could tell. James had composed nearly three hundred songs during his time in jail; maybe he'd promised them a backing track or two. They were heavy and surly in a way that Noodle didn't mind at all. His own date was an honest-to-goodness college girl from Medaille (he'd shown her his fake ID to prove he was going on twenty-two), but the James girls were about eighteen times more interesting. They looked as though they ate boys like Noodle for breakfast, raw and whole, with a chaser of lightbulbs and gin.

The house band was smoky and fierce—James came mostly for the music, though Noodle didn't know that yet—and the girl from Medaille (whose name was allegedly Delia) was clapping along, which was slightly embarrassing. Noodle didn't mind, though, or at least not too much, because it got the James posse's attention. He actually thought he saw James wink at him, though he had to admit to me, later, that it seemed unlikely. But that whole night was unlikely. Half an hour later, when Noodle went to the men's room, The Man Himself followed him in and took a long, hard leak into the next urinal over.

"Son," James said comfortably, "I'm going to make you a public service announcement."

"Excuse me?" said Noodle.

"That's a funky-ass cock you got there. It smells funny."

Noodle laughed tightly. Nothing in his life had prepared him for what was now happening.

"I mean that as a compliment," James assured him, blowing his nose into a satin handkerchief. "There's ladies I know—that I know *personally*—who appreciate a modicum of funk."

Before he could think of a reply, Noodle found himself alone again. But he'd barely returned to his seat—he hadn't even had time to tell Delia the story, not that she'd have believed him—when the first frosted pitcher of Michelob Dry arrived at their table. He knew who'd sent it without bothering to ask. Delia gazed at him with newfound admiration, until she realized that someone else had bought it. Then she got a faraway look in her eye. The next pitcher arrived before the first one was empty.

Looking back, Noodle could say with reasonable confidence that Delia was the true reason for James's largesse, but it wouldn't have mattered to him even if he'd known—and it certainly made no difference at the time. Delia must have sensed something, though, because she got spooked.

"Why does he keep sending pitchers?" she hissed at one point, when James had only sent two. "Jesus H." But she got used to the attention pretty quick. She clapped and smiled and waved past Noodle at The Man Himself's table. James smiled back, every inch the bourgeois cavalier, and tossed his Jheri curls in her direction. The women looked at Delia like she was one eyelash flutter shy of getting beat to shit. Delia actually seemed to like that too.

At the close of their set, the band—the William McKinleys—announced an after-hours appearance at the Grange Hole, an unlicensed club in a converted grain silo on the south side of town, a few blocks from the husked-out and junk-littered trench that had once been the Erie Canal. Chicken Noodle thought to himself—with a certain amount of relief—that there was no chance whatsoever that he'd be at the Grange Hole that night; but on this point he proved to be mistaken. They'd barely begun their third pitcher when James waved them over to his table. They hesitated a moment—longer than a moment; the better part of a minute, actually—then sheepishly, excitedly obliged.

"What's your name called, short greens?" James said to Delia. Noodle felt his skinny, snow-white body flicker and grow transparent.

"Mary Jane," Delia answered. Noodle was reasonably sure he'd never heard her call herself this before—he didn't know, at the time, that she was quoting one of James's more recent semihits. He began to doubt that she was actually enrolled at any college. She never so much as glanced at him again.

Fifteen minutes later the two of them were shoehorned into the back of a purple stretch LeSabre that felt a lot smaller than it looked from the outside, trying and failing to find something to talk about with Anne Hijazi, spouse and attaché and conscience of their host. The Man Himself was huddled at the front of the limousine's lounging/staging area with his two unnamed friends—he referred to them, for reasons unclear, as his "insurance policy"—and seemed to have forgotten about Delia and Noodle, at least for the moment. Anne Hijazi was staring at Delia as if she was trying to determine whether her skin would make a better jacket or a coat.

"I'm gonna be *you* tonight," Anne Hijazi whispered to Delia. "And you, Mary Jane—you is gonna be me."

It might simply have been the power of suggestion, but Chicken Noodle was struck, in that instant, by how much the two women resembled one another. Anne Hijazi could very well have looked like Delia before the freebase and the cigarette-burn torture and the eighteen months of prison; and Delia stood a very good chance, Noodle thought, of looking like Anne Hijazi in a few hard-lived years—maybe even by the end of that same night. He watched in a kind of idle, shitless stupor as Anne Hijazi and Delia traded jackets, then blouses, then certain other items of feminine apparel of whose purpose he was sadly unaware. According to testimony, a joint was lit and sucked on and passed forward. Noodle was reasonably sure that he saw The Man Himself *eat* it while it was still burning; his judgment may have been impaired, however, by Anne Hijazi's teeth, which had fastened themselves onto his left earlobe. *I'll have to remember this*, Noodle thought to himself through the coiling, shivering, luminescing fog. *Anne Hijazi is the one who bites.*

The scene inside the Grange had a single, vivid analogue in Noodle's young life. As a twelve-year-old kid he'd traveled to New York City with his mother: they were going to visit his sister at Columbia, a school he never had a prayer of attending himself. His mom was bad at maps, and Noodle was worse, and rather than take the A, C, E, they boarded a 3 train and got out at the 125th Street station. It was ten p.m. on a hot September night and everyone in the city was out on the street. Smoke and music and the smell of frying gristle filled the air. He hadn't felt threatened walking through Harlem at night with his mother— he'd felt irrelevant, which was exactly how he felt at the Grange. No one could care less that Chicken Noodle was there. He was seventh in line as they entered the club, but he might as well have been seven hundredth. He'd felt transparent before, watching James watching Delia; now he felt completely disembodied.

At some point, admittedly, he *did* smoke something that tasted like nothing he'd ever smoked or smelled or heard tell of before. It was less a taste at all, really, than a kind of angry, greasy pressure in his throat. It made his teeth feel soft and slightly furry. He threw up soon after, but enjoyed the experience. Someone took his wallet from his chinos and he didn't mind at all. Someone pulled off one of his Top-Siders, tried it on, then passed it back to him with a sigh. Someone asked him his opinion of the Bills' chances that season and he said the Bills could go suck their own dicks. The music dug into him and pinned him to the wall. He was high as hell, yes, but it was the *music*—Rick freaking James's music, music that seemed to belong to no one suddenly, to James himself least of all, and therefore, by Noodle's shattered, suicidal reasoning, could just as well have been his (Noodle's) own, up for grabs, free for the taking—that sparked and squirmed in our hero's modest brainstem and propelled him forward and under and finally up onto the creaking cinder-block-and-loading-pallet stage, behind The Man Himself, beside The Man Himself, then suddenly in the very spot The Man Himself had occupied: the piping, sweat-delineated, somehow blood-smelling locus of light and attention at the stage's precise geometric center, in the full upward thrust of the black-market kliegs, with the mic that James himself had just a moment before been brandishing and stroking and battering and sucking on like a vibrator or a lollipop or a probation officer's unlicensed Taser— the music that made it seem like a reasonable idea, after all he'd been through that hour and that night and in the course of his entire bland, tepid, milk-colored existence so far, to tip his head back and begin to sing.

"*She's a very kinky girl,*" sang Chicken Noodle, "*the kind you don't bring home to mother . . .*"

That's as far, by all reports, as he got.

PEACE BRIDGE

BY CONNIE PORTER

East Side

When I heard the noise, I reached for the gun. I mean, isn't that the purpose of having one, having it at hand? You keep it close by, so when you hear *that* noise in the middle of the night, the bungling burglar, the dog-footed cat thief, you can defend yourself; protect the sanctity of your cave.

My gun was on my nightstand—in my bedroom. I was across the hall in my office, a tiny bedroom that I hadn't gotten around to doing anything to since I had moved in a year ago, hunched over my laptop, on my third shot of espresso. The week before I'd had five shots, and I looked into the hallway at one point and swore I saw a circle of bluecaps dropping like it was hot.

Surreptitiously, as if the noise could see me, I snuck out my right pinkie to pause the dictation. It took me a few moments to recognize the piano music in "Moanin'" emerging into the room, white and cool and clean as a coast of gesso.

When I'm working, I play the jazz station softly. It's the only way I can transcribe the depositions. It keeps me in my chair, in my office, typing the details of yet another chicken-processing plant worker who had a finger sliced off while "disassembling" a chicken, or the line cook who suffered third-degree burns to both hands when the oil in a hundred-pound fryolator boiled over.

I don't hear the music. Consciously. It is translucent, light breathing life inside me. With the music, I inhale. I exhale, push my thoughts away from the voices, the names, the endless stream of blood keeping my lights on, keeping the collectors at bay.

I froze at the desk I had made out of cinder blocks and an old door I found in the basement, wondering if I had really heard anything. Mingus nimbly laid his bass line down, playing to me from beyond the veil. I could see his hands, his knuckles knobs of ginger, hot inside yet soothing. They reached out to comfort me where I sat while a trumpet laughed, *Wa-wa-wa!* Then, sliding right between the clapping of the hi-hat, there was *that* sound again. A groan rising from the warped floorboards of my dining room.

The closet was jammed with boxes of books and there was nowhere else to hide. If I'd bought the desk from Ikea instead of just bookmarking it in my browser, it would have been big and sturdy enough to hide under. Damn Peace! I had passed up the desk thinking of her. It was $279, and maybe I could have justified that for work, but there was no way in hell I could justify paying $349 to ship it to Buffalo, *New York*. Buffalo, Montana, maybe, but on the real, is Ikea outsourcing its shipping to Somali pirates? I was being responsible. I was being grown. I was the one thinking of someone, thinking of her while she was thinking of him. While she was with him. She was with him the last few months we lived together, I'm convinced of it. Gilles.

He's Haitian. Mr. *Exotique*. I used to be the exotic one, Lenny Kravitz with a twist—black father, Jewish mother. Peace used to love to play with my dreads, loved that I was a painter. Gilles's head is cleanly shaven, smooth and shiny as polished soapstone. He's getting a degree in communication and leadership at Canisius so he can return to Haiti and better serve his people.

She'd met him in early winter. Peace had wanted me to go to a fund-raiser for Haitian earthquake victims being held at a gallery in Allentown. She and her supervisor from the no-kill shelter were attending a silent auction and wine tasting. I knew the gallery; it was run by an older woman with wild green eyes and a spark of red hair. She looked like a wood sprite. I'd sold three paintings from my thesis, "The Color of Emotion"—*Crimson Staked Heart, Lavender Lust,* and *Fear of Love in Black and White*—but when I'd tried to show in her gallery, she turned me down.

When Peace came home from work and reminded me about the fund-raiser, I was just crawling out of the paxilated cave I had been in all day. Paxil, I'm convinced, was created by cavemen who go out and gather and hunt while you sit in darkness awaiting the spirit contained in the pill, tiny and blue as a robin's egg. Inside is the hope of warmth, unborn shadow, the joy and press of a woman against you in a corner of the night. But the hope and spirit never fully spark. All you get is smoke, a burning in the eyes, and the hard flint of promises that cannot ignite the wet tinder clotted in your heart.

I told Peace I wasn't going. "Figures," she said, still wrapped in layers and layers. She had walked from work, and it was snowing. "What do you do for anyone?"

I shouldn't have said anything. I was in no mood for her. I was in no mood, period. "What do *you* do that's so great?" I asked. "Take care of those wretched animals all day?"

Her cheeks were flooded with color, two lush blooms of Sarah Bernhardt peonies. "You should be grateful for those *wretched* animals because if it wasn't for them needing a place to stay, you wouldn't have a place to stay. They're feeding you. *I'm* feeding you! . . . You don't even paint anymore. All you do is make excuses. Your dad died. You're broke. You're blocked. No one wants to buy your work. What work?"

Canvases stood atop easels in the dining room of the apartment we shared, but I hadn't painted a stroke for months. I'd lost track of the days and nights of emptiness.

"You don't understand anything about what I do," I said defensively. The rectangular windows of whiteness stared at me, mocked me.

"I'm taking She-Ra with me," Peace said, grabbing the leash. "I wouldn't want her wretchedness spoiling your evening."

I didn't say anything. She-Ra was her dog, a pit bull–dachshund mix she had gotten from the shelter before we met. Most of the dogs at the shelter were pit bulls or pit bull mixes. When I used to pick Peace up from work, they barked like fiends from their wall of cages. The cats were in cages on the opposite wall, crouched, squint-eyed, gazing around suspiciously. Along the back wall there were small cages with fat, languid, pink-eyed rabbits that looked like they had been passing joints all day. Observing them all, I would wonder how it was discovered that they were unwanted. Who snitched on the stray cat? Didn't want to pat the bunny? Said that *one* bite from a pit bull was one too many? No matter when I went, the animals were always the same. Even when they weren't the same animals, they were the *same* animals. Peace was their savior, their jailer.

The night she went to the fund-raiser, I cried when she left, and took a pill hoping it would light my cave. I would cook breakfast for Peace in the morning. Take her to work. Pick her up. I would sleep all night, and in morning the light would be right for painting. The truth was, I was running out of the hope of light.

I had gotten my cache of Paxil from Mom. After Dad died, her doctor put her on it and while she settled his estate and slowly emerged from the shock of his sudden death, she had accumulated a half-dozen bottles of pills. She asked me to bring them to a drug take-back site over at the fairgrounds because she didn't want to flush them—that was bad for the fish, for the drinking water. I told her I would. I put the bag containing them into my car trunk and forgot about it until after the take-back was over. I then put them in my sock drawer. I would flush them. Mom would never know. I didn't care if the fish got drugged, and I only drank bottled water. And then there was this. This shadow, a streak of onyx pressing against my heart.

Dad had left me nothing. Mom was moving to Scottsdale and selling everything except a rental property on Jefferson Avenue. Dad owned it and four others sprinkled through the Fruit Belt, Cold Springs, Humboldt Park. Mom didn't feel up to maintaining them, and tracking down tenants for rent. The week after I got the Paxil, she called to tell me I could live in that house if I wanted. She would keep it in her name. All I had to do was pay the taxes on it and the utilities.

"If you can manage that for a year, I'll sign it over to you. You can do what you want with it then," Mom told me.

A brush of heat swept up my neck into my face. My forehead broke out in sweat. "If Dad wanted me to have a house, to have a . . . *anything*, he would have left it to me. He could have left me money. You can sell it and give me the money. I can use it to pay down my student loans."

Mom said coolly, "Let's be honest, it's going to take you a lifetime to pay them off."

"You sound like Dad!" I accused. "*You don't need a piece of paper to prove you're an artist*," I mimicked.

Mom stayed calm, stayed on track. "Has it ever occurred to you that your father was right? You should have never borrowed that kind of money for graduate school."

"I know how much I owe," I told her, though I had not told her, told Dad, told Peace, told anyone. The last bills I'd received— well, that I had opened—totaled $158,147.55.

"This isn't *Let's Make a Deal*, David. You're twenty-seven years old. You want to live in the house, or you don't. It's up to you. I can have my realtor put the house on Jefferson on the market too."

I was silent for a few moments, and then told Mom, "I need to talk it over with Peace first."

"Work things out with Peace. But as soon as the sale closes for this house, I'm leaving town."

When I picked Peace up from work, I told her about Mom's offer. She wanted to see the house.

"Why?" I asked. "It's just up the street from Gigi's. The East Side isn't safe."

We were stopped at a light. "Wait, so it's safe to go to a restaurant on the East Side, but not *live* over there? Thousands of people live there. You lived there as a kid."

"But I don't remember it. We moved to Orchard Park before I started kindergarten. People are always getting shot on the East Side. I mean, it's an *if it bleeds, it leads* gold mine for the evening news."

I hit the CD button. Teena Marie was holding a long "*loooooooove*," about to lay it down on Rick James. Peace punched it off. I punched it back on. Teena was still on the same note.

"Like no one gets shot on the West Side," she said as Teena, finishing the line, moaned softly.

"On the Puerto Rican West Side they do," I said. "Not where we live."

"Dude, you don't know how racist you sound!" Peace yelled. She had to duel with Teena, so I turned the player off this time and got blasted with a horn because the light had turned green.

"I'm not racist. How can I be racist? I come from the two most repressed people in the history of the planet," I insisted.

Peace was still screaming: "And the Irish have had it easy? Tell that to my grandparents. David, you're being a total tool. I wish my parents had money. Your mom's *giving* you a house and you don't want it!"

"With strings attached," I said. "I'm not a tool, and I'm definitely not a puppet. I'm not going to dance for her money—my dad's money either."

"Next month the rent's going up by fifty dollars. Do you have an extra fifty dollars a month? Do you have fifty dollars, period?" asked Peace.

My heartbeat went tribal. *Buppta, bupp, buppbuppbupp, buppta, bupp, buppbuppbupp.* Was this how it was with Dad? Driven out of this world by the runaway rhythm of a drummer's beat? I punched the CD player back on. Peace didn't reach over to stop Rick James from begging Teena to hold him one more time, to lie to him about everything being all right.

When the song wound down, I glanced at Peace and asked softly, "Are you all right?"

She was slunk down in her seat. She didn't say anything.

"I'd have to get a gun if we move to that house. I'd need one for protection."

"And you could kill someone? David, you won't even kill flies."

That was true. I didn't kill flies; I would release them out a window.

Peace spent all day rescuing animals, but let one fly get into the house and she would hunt it down and dispatch it into the next world with a flip-flop.

"I wouldn't be getting a gun to kill anyone. I would be getting it for, like I said, protection. We're not moving over there, so it's a moot point."

After a few minutes of silence, Peace said, "Dude, you're totally getting a job. Like yesterday."

Buppta, bupp

Peace probably would not have believed I was thinking of her as I flew across the hall and grabbed the gun from my nightstand, an upside-down milk crate. I had been meaning to stop by and see her all summer. Now it was turning fall. I slid out into the dark hallway and, putting winter in my voice, yelled down the stairs, "Get the hell out of my house or I'm going to shoot you!"

My voice echoed. The beating of my heart filled my ears. Rushing in between that sound was someone calling my name. I pressed my back against the wall, and listened to a small voice in the night.

"David, it's me! David! It's me. Malcolm. Don't shoot. It's Malcolm!"

I reached for the light switch and told him to turn on the light in the dining room. I heard him cross the creaking floor, and then saw the rush of light. "You're alone, aren't you?"

"I got my Xbox." He stood in my empty dining room, wearing a wifebeater and a pair of red, white, and blue Bills Zubaz. He didn't have anything on his feet, and he was holding the Xbox to his chest. A backpack was hanging from one shoulder.

"You know, you don't break into people's houses at three in the morning in this neighborhood, in *any* neighborhood, without risking getting shot."

Malcolm looked at me and a flood of words poured out: "I didn't break in, the back door was unlocked. I knocked on your front door because I seen a light was on upstairs and I could see you, and I called your name but not too loud because I ain't want my daddy to hear. So I went round back. My daddy, he put me out . . . Why you still holding the gun on me?"

I eyed Malcolm, eyed the gun in my hand. I had it pointed it at the floor. It's a BB gun identical to a police service pistol. When I was painting the mural on the side of house, I made a point of having it stuck just far enough outside my waistband to be seen by everyone, by anyone passing by. I wanted it to be known that I fit in here.

I don't know how much good a BB gun would have done with Malcolm. He's three hundred pounds, at least. I don't know how many times I would have had to shoot him, if I *had* to shoot him.

I was going to buy a real gun. That had been the plan. I priced a nine. Five hundred dollars. Even if I had scraped up the money to buy one, I would have wanted a permit to carry it concealed. The application for that is crazy. They wanted me to provide four character references, nonfamilial, the reason why I wanted to carry a concealed weapon, where I was going to keep it at home, if I was on medication, my work history, did I have any mental or emotional problems. Really, it's no wonder people buy illegal guns. I bought the BB gun on Amazon. Forty dollars, and the shipping was free.

I stuck the gun in my waistband. "Look, Malcolm, I'm not going to shoot you. I'm working. I'm sorry about your dad putting you out and everything. You can use my cell to call someone to come get you."

Malcolm started crying. I mean, no shame in his game. The kind of crying I did when I was four and Mom wouldn't buy me the Battle Armor Skeletor from the Hills Department Store because all she came in for was work socks for Dad. Malcolm cried like that, or maybe like I cried the day I moved out from Peace and into here. I left while she was at work, packed my entire life into my 2004 Ford Taurus. It only took me one trip.

"I don't got nobody to call," Malcolm said between sobs. "Daddy told me I have to get back in school, go in the morning, or I had to get out. And, and, and, I told him I wasn't going. Then he told me I got five minutes to pack. I grabbed this first." He patted the Xbox. "My grandmama gave it to me."

I had to get back to work so I could send off my transcription in the morning. I told him he could stay the night, sleep on the futon couch in the front room. "But you're going to have to go back home and work things out with your father in the morning."

Malcolm started crying again, this time more softly.

"Give me your backpack," I said.

He let it slide from his shoulder, and it hit the floor heavily.

I took it and led Malcolm to the couch. He plopped down in the middle of it. His nose was running, he was sweating. He wiped his face on his shirt. I could tell he was embarrassed. I didn't know what to say to him.

"I ain't going back to school. They mean to me, and they don't stop. I don't care what Daddy say. He don't have to hear it. They make fun of my name, and it ain't funny! They laugh, and it ain't funny!"

I leaned against the door trim and shook my head. "Where do you go to school?"

"East," he sniffled. "They don't act like they in high school. For real, they act like kids."

"They *are* kids. You're a kid. This is all going to pass by. It's going to be like a dream years from now. It won't matter . . . Look, I'm going to grab a quick coffee before I head back upstairs. You want one?"

Malcolm shook his head. "Can I hook up my Xbox to your TV?"

"I don't have one," I said, heading to the kitchen.

I turned on the light to see my back door was wide open. I shut it, locked it.

Malcolm had followed behind me. He asked, "Why not?

"Why not what?"

"You don't have a TV. Was you robbed? Ain't hardly nothing in here. Look like you was robbed," said Malcolm.

"No, I wasn't robbed. I don't own a TV."

"Me and Daddy got five. One in my room. His room. The living room. The kitchen. One in the bathroom . . . You was acting like I was breaking in here. Robin Hood the one need to be breaking in here so he can hook this place up."

I smiled when he said that. "I'm working on hooking it up. I'm buying myself a desk today," I told him.

I made myself a single, and frothed a cup of milk for Malcolm that drizzled with vanilla syrup. We returned to the living room because there wasn't anywhere else to sit, and Malcolm looked around at the walls.

He said, "You got a crazy man coming out your wall."

"That's Dr. Lonnie Smith," I told him. "And he's not crazy." I explained that he was a famous jazz musician, that he played the organ and was from Lackawanna.

"Is he a Muslim? He look like a Muslim. My mama left my daddy for a Muslim and he was crazy. They live in New York City now."

"He's Sikh," I said, looking at the regal blue turban. "That's a religion. The men don't cut their beards."

"Is he dead? My daddy say you painted Rick James because he was dead."

"Dr. Smith isn't dead. Not that I know of, and I don't remember saying that," I replied, sipping my coffee. "About Rick James. Exactly."

It was the beginning of summer in Buffalo when I moved in here, a season of light. I sat up nights working, and it was just as well. I couldn't sleep. I was coming down off the Paxil. I'd finish up around seven, having seen the light before the sun itself. Potter's pink, cadmium orange. I couldn't stand it, the beauty of the clouds painted so hopefully, the grace of green leaves emerging from darkness in the tree outside my window, stretching beyond the roofline. I didn't have money for curtains, so I put aluminum foil up on my bedroom windows. It blocked the coming of the light. Even having been up all night, I could hardly sleep during the day. When I did, I would fall asleep briefly and have nightmares. I couldn't remember the details, but I would wake with my tribal heart. In my cave. Stalked by shadows, by spirits of the slipped and fallen, the quick and the dead.

One morning, without ever remembering I slept, I woke with a shaft of life piercing my left eye. The foil had peeled back from one of the panes, and in it, standing in the midst of the leaves, was Horus. His bronze body was lean and muscled. His black hawk's head was adorned with a crown, and he had a mass of braids spilling down his back. His all-seeing eye looked out at me.

I sat up, not afraid, expecting him to speak to me. He didn't say a word. He vanished. Then I woke up. Again. Not sure what was real. Which world was the dream. I was lying on the floor. I didn't have a bed yet, only a sleeping bag. The foil on the windows was all intact. I peeled it off, and sitting in the tree was a huge black crow. It cawed and flew off into the blue.

I stood up then. I shopped all day. I bought gallons of paint, a ladder, and the next morning after I e-mailed in my work, I went outside. With my gun in my pants, I began painting the south wall of my house.

I started with the body, worked on it for weeks, as a small creep of heat pushed into the days. I sweated, and felt dizzy at times when I climbed on the ladder to complete the chest and arms. As the sun lifted in the sky, teenage boys would come up the street bouncing basketballs loudly. I would watch them out of the corner of an eye. By the time I got to the hair on the mural, I had a clearer head and an audience. Malcolm and his father would sit on the porch across the street and watch me. They ate breakfast out there, and Malcolm's father had a speaker from a stereo in the window and would play Harold Melvin and the Blue Notes, Rick James, Phyllis Hyman, Donny Hathaway, Marvin Gaye, Grover Washington. A choir of the dead.

One morning, I had come down off the ladder and was sipping a cup of coffee on the front porch when Malcolm and his father walked across the street and introduced themselves. Malcolm then promptly went back across the street and disappeared into the house.

His father sat on the bottom step. "He's good, my boy. Tenderhearted. He like your painting. Your work do look good, but you gonna put some sandals on him, right? He wore sandals."

"Horus, oh, he was always barefooted. At least from what I've seen."

"Who, was he in Earth, Wind & Fire? Them brothers always liked to dress like they just fell out a boat in the Nile River."

."No," I explained, my tongue clumsy. I hadn't talked in a month. "He's, umm, a spirit. An Egyptian god. When you paint, sometimes ideas come to you. You dream them. They dream you. Spirits."

"Damn, I'm wrong, I been telling Malcolm that was Rick James you was painting. I was sure of it when I seen them braids. The *Throwin' Down* album cover, except Rick didn't wear that skirt thing you had him in. He had on a loincloth."

"Hmmm," I said.

"Hey, you the painter. I'm not. I got it all wrong."

"No, no, you didn't get it wrong. There's no getting it wrong," I said. "Maybe they are the same spirit."

"If you looking for some spirits, all kinds of spirits around here." He waved his arms. "Rick around here, still. He grew up around here, partied around here, even when he was famous. I seen him once when I was a kid. Right here on Jefferson. He signed autographs for anyone who wanted one. I got one, but I lost it. It was just on a little piece of paper. But anyway, I'ma let you get back to work. I ain't got to be to work until three." He got up from the porch.

As he headed across the street, I asked, "Do you want me to make it Rick? I haven't done the head yet."

He turned around, smiling broadly. "You serious?"

I nodded.

"Make it Rick, then," he said, "and I'ma tell Malcolm I was right. Ain't too many times a boy think his daddy is right about nothing. Deuces!" He flashed two fingers at me.

"Deuces!" I said in turn.

This house I sat in, with Malcolm, with my fake gun, was mine, officially mine, my cave. My real home. Mom had signed it over to me, just as she had promised.

When I had looked at the permit-to-carry application, there was one section that stopped me cold. Who would safeguard my gun if I died? I had no answer, and a part of me, a part I had buried in darkness, realized I had no one to protect me from the gun I wanted to hide. Who would protect me when the weight of darkness was too great?

"I'm painting Harold Arlen next," I told Malcolm. "I'm putting him outside on the opposite side of the house from Rick. He's from Buffalo too. He wrote 'Over the Rainbow.'"

"My grandmama loved that song," said Malcolm. "They played it at her funeral and it was like Patti LaBelle was really up in the church with us. My grandmama loved her. When Patti would kick her shoes off and flap like a bird, my grandmama would say she was struck by the spirit."

"Look," I said, getting up, "I'll go with you to talk to your dad in morning, if you want me to."

"Maybe he'll listen to you. He like you."

"I don't know about that. All I can say is, I'm sure he wants what's best for you."

Malcolm nodded his head. "You hear that music? It's spooky up in here."

"That's just the radio," I said. "I left it on upstairs."

"Can I leave the lights on?"

"Yes," I said. "Yes," and I headed up the stairs.

PART III

BLOODLINES

VALENTINE

BY JOYCE CAROL OATES

Delaware Park

I n upstate New York in those years there were snowstorms
so wild and fierce they could change the world, within a
few hours, to a place you wouldn't know. First came the
heavy black thunderheads over Lake Erie, then the wind ham-
mering overhead like a freight train, then the snowflakes erupt-
ing, flying, swirling like crazed atoms. If there'd been a sun it
was extinguished, gone. Night and day were reversed, the fallen
snow emitted such a radium glare.

I was fifteen years old living in the Red Rock section of
Buffalo with an aunt, an older sister of my mother's, and her
husband who was retired from the New York Central Railroad with a disability pension. My own family was what you'd
called "dispersed"—we were all alive, seven of us, I believed we
were all alive, but we did not live together in the same house any
longer. In fact, the house, an old rented farmhouse twenty miles
north of Buffalo, was gone. Burned to the ground.

Valentine's Day 1959, the snowstorm began in midafternoon
and already by five p.m. the power lines were down in the city.
Hurriedly we lit kerosene lamps whose wicks smoked and stank
as they gave off a begrudging light. We had a flashlight, of course,
and candles. In extra layers of clothes we saw our breaths steam
as we ate our cold supper on plates like ice. I cleaned up the
kitchen as best I could without hot water, for that was always
my task, among numerous others, and I said "Goodnight, Aunt
Esther" to my aunt who frowned at me, seeing someone not-me
in my place who filled her heart with sisterly sorrow, and I said

"Goodnight, Uncle Herman" to the man designated as my uncle, who was no blood-kin of mine, a stranger with damp eyes always drifting onto me and a mouth like a smirking scar burn. "Goodnight" they murmured as if resenting the very breath expelled for my sake. *Goodnight, don't run on the stairs, don't drop the candle and set the house on fire.*

Upstairs was a partly finished attic narrow as a tunnel with a habitable space at one end—my "room." The ceiling was covered in strips of peeling insulation and so steep-slanted I could stand up only in the center. The floorboards were splintery and bare except for a small shag rug, a discard of my aunt's, laid down by my bed. The bed was another discard of my aunt's, a sofa of some mud-brown prickly fabric that pierced sheets laid upon it like whiskers sprouting through skin. But this was *a bed of my own* and I had not ever had *a bed of my own* before. Nor had I ever had *a room of my own, a door to shut against others,* even if, like the attic door, it could not be locked.

By midnight the storm had blown itself out and the alley below had vanished in undulating dunes of snow. Everywhere snow! Glittering like mica in the moonlight! And the moon—a glowing battered-human face in a sky strangely starless, black as a well. The largest snowdrift I'd ever seen, shaped like a right-angled triangle, slanted up from the ground to the roof close outside the window. My aunt and her husband had gone to bed downstairs hours ago and the thought came to me unbidden: *I can run away, no one would miss me.*

Along Huron Street, which my aunt's house fronted, came a snowplow; red light flashing atop its cab; otherwise there were few vehicles and these were slow-moving with groping head-lights, like wounded beasts. Yet even as I watched there came a curiously shaped small vehicle to park at the mouth of the alley; and the driver, a long-legged man in a hooded jacket, climbed out. To my amazement he stomped through the snow into the alley to stand peering up toward my window, his breath steaming. Who? Who was this? *Mr. Lacey, my algebra teacher?*

For Valentine's Day that morning I had brought eight homemade valentines to school made of stiff red construction paper edged with paper lace, in envelopes decorated with red-ink hearts; the valentine *TO MR. LACEY* was my masterpiece, the largest and most ingeniously designed, interlocking hearts fashioned with a ruler and compass to resemble geometrical figures in three dimensions. *HAPPY VALENTINE'S DAY*, I had neatly printed in black ink. Of course I had not signed any of the valentines and had secretly slipped them into the lockers of certain girls and boys and Mr. Lacey's onto his desk after class. I had instructed myself not to be disappointed when I received no valentines in return, not a single valentine in return, and I was not disappointed when at the end of the school day I went home without a single one: *I was not.*

Mr. Lacey seemed to have recognized me in the window where I stood staring, my outspread fingers on the glass bracketing my white astonished face, for he'd begun climbing the enormous snowdrift that lifted to the roof! How assured, how matter-of-fact, as if this were the most natural thing in the world. I was too surprised to be alarmed, or even embarrassed—my teacher would see me in a cast-off sweater of my brother's that was many sizes too large for me and splotched with oil stains, he would see my shabby little room that wasn't really a room, just part of an unfinished attic. He would know I was the one who'd left the valentine *TO MR. LACEY* on his desk in stealth, not daring to sign my name. *He would know who I was, how desperate for love.*

Once on the roof, which was steep, Mr. Lacey made his way to my window cautiously. The shingles were covered in snow, icy patches beneath. There was a rumor that Mr. Lacey was a skier, and a skater, though his lanky body did not seem the body of an athlete, and in class sometimes he seemed distracted in the midst of speaking or inscribing an equation on the blackboard; as if there were thoughts more crucial to him than tenth-grade algebra at Thomas E. Dewey High School, which was one of the poorest schools in the city. But now his footing was sure as a mountain goat's, his movements agile and unerring. He crouched outside my window tugging to lift it—*Erin? Make haste!*

I was helping to open the window which was locked in ice. It had not been opened for weeks. Already it seemed I'd pulled on my wool slacks and wound around my neck the silver muffler threaded with crimson yarn my mother had given me two or three Christmases ago. I had no coat or jacket in my room and dared not risk going downstairs to the front closet. I was very excited, fumbling, biting my lower lip, and when at last the window lurched upward, the freezing air rushed in like a slap in the face. Mr. Lacey's words seemed to reverberate in my ears: *Make haste, make haste!—not a moment to waste!* It was his teasing-chiding classroom manner that nonetheless meant business. Without hesitating, he grabbed both my hands—I saw that I was wearing the white angora mittens my grandmother had knitted for me long ago, which I'd believed had been lost in the fire—and hauled me through the window.

Mr. Lacey led me to the edge of the roof, to the snowdrift, seeking out his footprints where he knew the snow to be fairly firm, and carefully he pulled me in his wake so that I seemed to be descending a strange kind of staircase. The snow was so fresh-fallen it lifted like powder at the slightest touch or breath, glittering even more fiercely close up, as if the individual snowflakes, of such geometrical beauty and precision, contained minute sparks of flame. *Er-in, Er-in, now your courage must begin,* I seemed to hear, and suddenly we were on the ground and there was Mr. Lacey's Volkswagen at the mouth of the alley, headlights burning like cat's eyes and tusks of exhaust curling up behind. How many times covertly I'd tracked with my eyes that ugly-funny car shaped like a sardine can, its black chassis speckled with rust, as Mr. Lacey drove into the teachers' parking lot each morning between 8:25 and 8:35 a.m. How many times I'd turned

quickly aside in terror that Mr. Lacey would see *me*. Now I stood
confused at the mouth of the alley, for Huron Street and all of
the city I could see was so changed, the air so terribly cold like
a knifeblade in my lungs; I looked back at the darkened house
wondering if my aunt might wake and discover me gone, and
what then would happen?—as Mr. Lacey urged, *Come, Erin,
hurry! She won't even know you're gone,* unless he said, *She won't
ever know you're gone.* Was it true? Not long ago in algebra class
I'd printed in the margin of my textbook,

MR.
L.
IS
AL
WA
YS
RI
GH
T!

which I'd showed Linda Bewley across the aisle, one of the
popular tenth-grade girls, a B+ student and very pretty and popular, and Linda frowned trying to decipher the words which were
meant to evoke Mr. Lacey's pole-lean frame, but she never did
get it and turned away from me annoyed.

Yet it was so: Julius Lacey was always always right.

Suddenly I was in the cramped little car and Mr. Lacey was
behind the wheel driving north on icy Huron Street. *Where are
we going?* I didn't dare ask. When my grades in Mr. Lacey's class
were less than 100 percent I was filled with anxiety that turned
my fingers and toes to ice, for even if I'd answered nearly all the
questions on a test correctly, *how could I know I could answer
the next question? solve the next problem? and the next?* A nervous
passion drove me to comprehend not just the immediate prob-

lem but the principle behind it, for behind everything there was an elusive and tyrannical principle of which Mr. Lacey was the sole custodian; and I could not know if he liked me or was bemused by me or merely tolerated me or was in fact disappointed in me as a student who should have been earning perfect scores at all times. He was twenty-six or -seven years old, the youngest teacher at the school, whom many students feared and hated, and a small group of us feared and admired. His severe, angular face registered frequent dissatisfaction as if to indicate, *Well, I'm waiting! Waiting to be impressed! Give me one good reason to be impressed!*

Never had I seen the city streets so deserted. Mr. Lacey drove no more than twenty miles an hour passing stores whose fronts were obliterated by snow like waves frozen at their crests and through intersections where no traffic lights burned to guide us and our only light was the Volkswagen's headlights and the glowering moon large in the sky as a fat navel orange held at arm's length. We passed Carthage Street that hadn't yet been plowed—a vast river of snow six feet high. We passed Templeau Street where a city bus had been abandoned in the intersection, humped with snow like a forlorn creature of the Great Plains. We passed Sturgeon Street where broken electrical wires writhed and crackled in the snow like snakes crazed with pain. We passed Childress Street where a water main had burst and an arc of water had frozen glistening in a graceful curve at least fifteen feet high at its crest. At Ontario Avenue Mr. Lacey turned right, the Volkswagen went into a delirious skid, Mr. Lacey put out his arm to keep me from pitching forward—*Erin, take care!* But I was safe. And on we drove.

Ontario Avenue, usually so crowded with traffic, was deserted as the surface of the moon. A snowplow had forged a single lane down the center. On all sides were unfamiliar shapes of familiar objects engulfed in snow and ice—parking meters? mailboxes? abandoned cars? humanoid figures frozen in awkward, surprised postures—hunched in doorways, frozen in mid-stride on the sidewalk? *Look! Look at the frozen people!* I cried in a raw loud girl's voice that so frequently embarrassed me when Mr. Lacey called upon me unexpectedly in algebra class; but Mr. Lacey shrugged, saying, *Just snowmen, Erin—don't give them a second glance.* But I couldn't help staring at these statue-figures for I had an uneasy sense of being stared at by them in turn, through chinks in the hard-crusted snow of their heads. And I seemed to hear their faint despairing cries—*Help! help us!*—but Mr. Lacey did not slacken his speed.

(Yet: who could have made so many "snowmen" so quickly after the storm? Children? Playing so late at night? And where were these children now?)

Mysteriously Mr. Lacey said, *There are many survivors, Erin. In all epochs, just enough survivors.* I wanted to ask, *Should we pray for them?* pressing my hands in the angora mittens against my mouth to keep from crying, for I knew how hopeless prayer was in such circumstances, God only helps those who don't require His help.

Were we headed for the lakefront?—we crossed a swaying bridge high above railroad tracks, and almost immediately after that another swaying bridge high above an ice-locked canal. We passed factories shut down by the snowstorm with smoke-stacks so tall their rims were lost in mist. We were on South Main Street now passing darkened shuttered businesses, ware-houses, a slaughterhouse; windowless brick buildings against whose walls snow had been driven as if sandblasted in eerie, almost legible patterns. These were messages, I was sure!—yet I could not read them. Out of the corner of my eye I watched Mr. Lacey as he drove. We were close together in the cramped car; yet at the same time I seemed to be watching us from a distance. At school there were boys who were fearful of Mr. Lacey yet, behind his back, sneered at him muttering what they'd like to do with him, slash his car tires, beat him up, and I felt a thrill of satisfaction, *If you could see Mr. Lacey now!* for he was navigating the Volkswagen so capably along the treacherous street, past snowy hulks of vehicles abandoned by the wayside. He'd shoved back the hood of his wool jacket—how handsome he looked! Where by day he often squinted behind his glasses, by night he seemed fully at ease. His hair was long and quill-like and of the subdued brown hue of a deer's winter coat; his eyes, so far as I could see, had a luminous coppery sheen. I recalled how at the high school Mr. Lacey was regarded with doubt and unease by the other teachers, many of whom were old enough to be his parents; he was considered arrogant because he didn't have an education degree from a state teachers' college like the others, but a master's degree in math from the University of Buffalo where he was a part-time PhD student. *Maybe I will reap where I haven't had any luck sowing,* he'd once remarked to the class, standing chalk in hand at the blackboard which was covered in calculations. And this remark too had passed over our heads.

Now Mr. Lacey was saying as if bemused, *Here, Erin—the edge. We'll go no farther in this direction.* For we were at the shore of Lake Erie—a frozen lake drifted in snow so far as the eye could see. (Yet I seemed to know how beneath the ice the water was agitated as if boiling, sinuous and black as tar.) Strewn along the beach were massive ice boulders that glinted coldly in the moonlight. Even by day at this edge of the lake you could see only an edge of the Canadian shore, the farther western shore was lost in distance. I was in terror that Mr. Lacey out of some whim would abandon me here, for never could I have made my way back to my aunt's house in such cold.

But already Mr. Lacey was turning the car around, already we were driving inland, a faint tinkling music seemed to draw us, and within minutes we were in a wooded area I knew to be Delaware Park—though I'd never been there before. I had heard my classmates speak of skating parties here and had yearned to be invited to join them as I had yearned to be invited to visit the homes of certain girls, without success. *Hang on! Hang on!* Mr. Lacey said, for the Volkswagen was speeding like a sleigh on curving lanes into the interior of a deep evergreen forest. And suddenly—we were at a large oval skating rink above which strings of starry lights glittered like Christmas bulbs, where dozens, hundreds of elegantly dressed skaters circled the ice as if there had never been any snowstorm, or any snowstorm that mattered to *them*. Clearly these were privileged people, for electric power had been restored for their use and burned brilliantly, wastefully on all sides. *Oh, Mr. Lacey, I've never seen anything so beautiful,* I said, biting my lip to keep from crying. It was a magical, wondrous place—the Delaware Park skating rink! Skaters on ice smooth as glass—skating round and round to gay, amplified music like that of a merry-go-round. Many of the skaters were in brightly colored clothes, handsome sweaters, fur hats, fur muffs; beautiful dogs of no breed known to me trotted alongside their masters and mistresses, pink tongues lolling in contentment. There were angel-faced girls in skaters' costumes, snug little pearl-buttoned velvet jackets and flouncy skirts to midthigh, gauzy knit stockings and kidskin boot-skates with blades that flashed like sterling silver—my heart yearned to see such skates for I'd learned to skate on rusted old skates formerly belonging to my older sisters, on a creek near our farmhouse; in truth I had never really learned to skate, not as these skaters were skating, so without visible effort, strife, or anxiety. Entire families were skating—mothers and fathers hand in hand with small children, and older children, and white-haired elders who must have been grandparents!—and the family dog trotting along with that look of dogs laughing. There were attractive young people in groups, and couples with their arms around each other's waists, and solitary men and boys who swiftly threaded their way through the crowd unerring as undersea creatures perfectly adapted to their element. Never would I have dared join these skaters, except Mr. Lacey insisted. Even as I feebly protested, *Oh, but I can't, Mr. Lacey—I don't know how to skate,* he was pulling me to the skate rental where he secured a pair of skates for each of us; and suddenly there I was stumbling and swaying in the presence of real skaters, my ankles weak as water and my face blotched with embarrassment, oh what a spectacle—but Mr. Lacey had closed his fingers firmly around mine and held me upright, refused to allow me to fall. *Do as I do! Of course you can skate! Follow me!* So I had no choice but to follow, like an unwieldy lake barge hauled by a tugboat.

How loud the happy tinkling music was out on the ice, far louder than it had seemed on shore, as the lights too were brighter, nearly blinding. *Oh! Oh!* I panted in Mr. Lacey's wake, terrified of slipping and falling; breaking a wrist, an arm, a leg; terrified of falling in the paths of swift skaters whose blades flashed sharp and cruel as butcher knives. Everywhere was a harsh hissing sound of blades sliced the surface of the ice, a sound you couldn't hear on shore. I would be cut to ribbons if I fell! All my effort was required simply to stay out of the skaters' paths as they flew by, with no more awareness of me than if I were a passing shadow; the only skaters who noticed me were children, girls as well as boys, already expert skaters as young as nine or ten who glanced at me with smiles of bemusement, or disdain. *Out! out of our way! you don't belong here on our ice!* But I was stubborn too, I persevered, and after two or three times around the rink I was still upright and able to skate without Mr. Lacey's continuous vigilance, my head high and my arms extended for balance. My heart beat in giddy elation and pride. I was skating! At last! Mr. Lacey dashed off to the center of the ice where more practiced skaters performed, executing rapid circles, figure eights, dancer-like and acrobatic turns, his skate blades flashing, and a number of onlookers applauded, as I applauded, faltering but regaining my balance, skating on. I was not graceful—not by any stretch of the imagination—and I guessed I must have looked a sight, in an old baggy oil-stained sweater and rumpled wool slacks, my kinky-snarly red-brown hair in my eyes—but I wasn't quite so clumsy any longer, my ankles were getting stronger and the strokes of my skate blades more assured, sweeping. How happy I was! How proud! I was beginning to be warm, almost feverish inside my clothes.

Restless as a wayward comet, a blinding spotlight moved about the rink singling out skaters, among them Mr. Lacey as he spun at the very center of the rink, an unlikely, storklike figure to be so graceful on the ice; for some reason then the spotlight abruptly shifted—to me! I was so caught by surprise I nearly tripped and fell—I heard applause, laughter—saw faces at the edge of the rink grinning at me. Were they teasing, or sincere? Kindly, or cruel? I wanted to believe they were kindly for the rink was such a happy place, but I couldn't be sure as I teetered past, arms flailing to keep my balance. I couldn't be certain but I seemed to see some of my high school classmates among the spectators; and some of my teachers; and others, adults, a case-worker from the Erie County family services department, staring at me disapprovingly. The spotlight was tormenting me: rushing at me, then falling away; allowing me to skate desperately on-ward, then seeking me out again swift and pitiless as a cheetah in pursuit of prey. The harshly tinkling music ended in a burst of static as if a radio had been turned violently up, then off. A sudden vicious wind rushed thin and sharp as a razor across the ice. My hair whipped in the wind, my ears were turning to ice. My fingers in the tight angora mittens were turning to ice too. Most of the skaters had gone home, I saw to my disappointment, the better-dressed, better-mannered skaters, all the families, and the only dogs that remained were wild-eyed mongrels with bris-tling hackles and stumpy tails. Mr. Lacey and I skated hastily to a deserted snowswept section of the rink to avoid these dogs, and were pursued by the damned spotlight; here the ice was rippled and striated and difficult to skate on. An arm flashed at the edge of the rink, I saw a jeering white face, and an ice-packed snowball came flying to strike Mr. Lacey between his shoulder blades and shatter in pieces to the ground. Furious, his face reddening, Mr. Lacey whirled in a crouch—*Who did that? Which of you?* He spoke with his classroom authority but he wasn't in his classroom now and the boys only mocked him more insolently. They chanted something that sounded like, *Lac-ey! Lac-ey! Ass-y! Assy-asshole!* Another snowball struck him on the side of the head, sending his glasses flying and skittering along the ice. I shouted for them to *stop! stop!* and a snowball came careening past my head, another struck my arm, hard. Mr. Lacey shook his fist, daring to move toward our attackers, but this only unleashed a new barrage of snowballs; several struck him with such force he was knocked down, a starburst of red at his mouth. Without his glasses Mr. Lacey looked young as a boy himself, dazed and helpless. On my hands and knees I crawled across the ice to retrieve his glasses, thank God there was only a hairline crack on one of the lenses. I was trembling with anger, sobbing. I was sure I recognized some of the boys, boys in my algebra class, but I didn't know their names. I crouched over Mr. Lacey asking was he all right? was he all right? seeing that he was stunned, pressing a handkerchief against his bleeding mouth. It was one of his white cotton handkerchiefs he'd take out of a pocket in class, shake ceremoniously open, and use to polish his glasses. The boys trotted away jeering and laughing. Mr. Lacey and I were alone, the only skaters remaining on the rink. Even the mongrels had departed.

It was very cold now. Earlier that day there'd been a warning—temperatures in the Lake Erie–Lake Ontario region would drop as low that night, counting the windchill factor, as -30 degrees Fahrenheit. The wind stirred snake-skeins of powdery snow as if the blizzard might be returning. Above the rink most of the lightbulbs had burnt out or had been shattered by the rising wind. The fresh-fallen snow that had been so purely white was now trampled and littered; dogs had urinated on it; strewn about were cigarette butts, candy wrappers, lost boots, mittens, a wool knit cap. My pretty handknit muffler lay on the ground stiffened with filth—one of the jeering boys must have taken it from me when I was distracted. I bit my lip to keep from crying, the muffler had been ruined and I refused to pick it up. Subdued, silent, Mr. Lacey and I hunted our boots amid the litter, and left our skates behind in a slovenly mound, and limped back to the Volkswagen that was the only vehicle remaining in the snow-swept parking lot. Mr. Lacey swore seeing the front windshield had been cracked like a spiderweb, very much as the left lens of his glasses had been cracked. Ironically he said, *Now you know, Erin, where the Delaware Park skating rink is.*

The bright battered-face moon had sunk nearly to the treeline, about to be sucked into blankest night.

In the Bison City Diner adjacent to the Greyhound bus station on Eighth Street, Mr. Lacey and I sat across a booth from each other, and he gave our order to a brassy-haired waitress in a terse mutter—*Two coffees, please.* Stern and frowning to discourage the woman from inquiring after his reddened face and swollen, still bleeding mouth. And then he excused himself to use the men's room. My bladder was aching, I had to use the restroom as well, but would have been too shy to slip out of the booth if Mr. Lacey hadn't gone first.

It was three twenty a.m. So late! The electricity had been restored in parts of Buffalo, evidently—driving back from the park we saw streetlights burning, traffic lights again operating. Still, most of the streets were deserted; choked with snow. The only other vehicles were snowplows and trucks spewing salt on the streets. Some state maintenance workers were in the Bison Diner, which was a twenty-four-hour place, seated at the counter, talking and laughing loudly together and flirting with the waitress who knew them. When Mr. Lacey and I came into the brightly lit room, blinking, no doubt somewhat dazed-looking, the men glanced at us curiously but made no remarks. At least, none that we could hear. Mr. Lacey touched my arm and gestured with his head for me to follow him to a booth in the farthest corner of the diner—as if it was the most natural thing in the world, the two of us sliding into that very booth.

In the clouded mirror in the women's room I saw my face strangely flushed, eyes shining like glass. This was a face not exactly known to me; more like my older sister Janice's, yet not Janice's either. I cupped cold water into my hands and lowered my face to the sink, grateful for the water's coolness since my skin was feverish and prickling. My hair was matted as if someone had used an eggbeater on it and my sweater, my brother's discard, was more soiled than I'd known, unless some of the stains were blood—for maybe I'd gotten Mr. Lacey's blood on me out on the ice. *Er-in Don-egal*, I whispered aloud in awe, amazement. In wonder. Yes, in pride! I was fifteen years old.

Inspired, I searched through my pockets for my tube of raspberry lipstick, and eagerly dabbed fresh color on my mouth. The effect was instantaneous. *Barbaric!* I heard Mr. Lacey's droll voice for so he'd once alluded to female "makeup" in our class, *Painting faces like savages with a belief in magic.* But he'd only been joking.

I did believe in magic, I guess. I had to believe in something!

When I returned to the booth in a glow of self-consciousness, there was Mr. Lacey with his face freshly washed too, and his lank hair dampened and combed. His part was on the left side of his head, and wavery. He squinted up at me—his face pinched in a quick frowning smile signaling he'd noticed the lipstick, but certainly wouldn't comment on it. Pushed a menu in my direction— *Order anything you wish, Erin, you must be starving*—and I picked it up to read it, for in fact I was light-headed with hunger, but the print was blurry as if under water and to my alarm I could not decipher a word. In regret I shook my head no, no thank you. *No, Erin? Nothing?* Mr. Lacey asked, surprised. Elsewhere in the diner a jukebox was playing a sentimental song—"Are You Lonesome Tonight?" At the counter, amid clouds of cigarette smoke, the workmen and the brassy-haired waitress erupted in laughter.

It seemed that Mr. Lacey had left his bloody handkerchief in the car and, annoyed and embarrassed, was dabbing at his mouth with a wadded paper towel from the men's room. His upper lip was swollen as if a bee had stung it and one of his front teeth was loose in its socket and still leaked blood. Almost inaudibly he whispered, *Damn. Damn. Damn.* His coppery-brown eye through the cracked left lens of his glasses was just perceptibly magnified and seemed to be staring at me with unusual intensity. I shrank before the man's gaze for I feared he blamed me as the source of his humiliation and pain. In truth, I *was* to blame: these things would never have happened to Julius Lacey except for me.

Yet when Mr. Lacey spoke it was with surprising kindness. Asking, *Are you sure you want nothing to eat, Erin? Nothing, nothing—at all?*

I could have devoured a hamburger half raw, and a plate of greasy french fries heaped with ketchup, but there I was shaking my head, *No, no thank you, Mr. Lacey.*

Why? I was stricken with self-consciousness, embarrassment. To eat in the presence of this man! The intimacy would have been paralyzing, like stripping myself naked before him.

Indeed it was awkward enough when the waitress brought us our coffee, which was black, hotly steaming in thick mugs. Once or twice in my life I'd tried to drink coffee, for everyone seemed to drink it, and the taste was repulsive to me, so bitter! But now I lifted the mug to my lips and sipped timidly at the steaming-hot liquid black as motor oil. Seeing that Mr. Lacey disdained to add dairy cream or sugar to his coffee, I did not add any to my own. I was already nervous and almost at once my heart gave odd erratic beats and my pulse quickened.

One of my lifetime addictions, to this bitterly black steaming-hot liquid, would begin at this hour, in such innocence.

Mr. Lacey was saying with an air of reluctance, finality, *In every equation there is always an X factor, and in every X factor there is the possibility, if not the probability, of tragic misunderstanding.* Out of his jacket pocket he'd taken, to my horror, a folded sheet of paper—red construction paper!—and was smoothing it out on the tabletop. I stared, I was speechless with chagrin. *You must not offer yourself in such a fashion, not even in secret, anonymously,* Mr. Lacey said with a teacher's chiding frown. *The valentine heart is the female genitals, you will be misinterpreted.*

There was a roaring in my ears confused with music from the jukebox. The bitter black coffee scalded my throat and began to race along my veins. Words choked me, *I'm sorry. I don't know what that is. Don't know what you're speaking of. Leave me alone, I hate you!* But I could not speak, just sat there shrinking to make myself as small as possible in Mr. Lacey's eyes, staring with a pretense of blank dumb ignorance at the elaborate geometrical valentine *TO MR. LACEY* I had made with such hope the other night in the secrecy of my room, knowing I should not commit such an audacious act yet also knowing, with an almost unbearable excitement, like one bringing a lighted match to flammable material, that I was going to do it.

Resentfully I said, *I guess you know about me, my family. I guess there aren't any secrets.*

Mr. Lacey said, *Yes, Erin. There are no secrets. But it's our prerogative not to speak of them if we choose.* Carefully he was refolding the valentine to return to his pocket, which I interpreted as a gesture of forgiveness. He said, *There is nothing to be ashamed of, Erin. In you, or in your family.*

Sarcastically I said, *There isn't?*

Mr. Lacey said, *The individuals who are your mother and father came together out of all the universe to produce you. That's how you came into being, there was no other way.*

I couldn't speak, I was struck dumb. Wanting to protest, to laugh, but could not. Hot tears ran down my cheeks.

Mr. Lacey persisted, gravely, *And you love them, Erin. Much more than you love me.*

Mutely I shook my head no.

Mr. Lacey said, with his air of completing an algebra problem on the blackboard, in a tone of absolute finality, *Yes. And we'll never speak of it again after tonight. In fact, of any of this*—making an airy magician's gesture that encompassed not just the Bison Diner but the city of Buffalo, the very night—*ever again.*

And so it was, we never did speak of it again—our adventure that night following Valentine's Day 1959—ever again.

Next Monday at school, and all the days and months to come, Mr. Lacey and I maintained our secret. My heart burned with a knowledge I could not speak! But I was quieter, less nervous in class than I'd ever been; as if, overnight, I'd matured by years. Mr. Lacey behaved exactly, I think, as he'd always behaved toward me: no one could ever have guessed, in any wild flight of imagination, the bond between us. My grades hovered below 100 percent, for Mr. Lacey was surely one to wish to retain the power of giving tests no student could complete to perfection. With a wink he said, *Humility goeth in place of a fall, Erin.* And in September when I returned for eleventh grade, Julius Lacey, who might have been expected to teach solid geometry to my class, was gone: returned to graduate school, we were told. Vanished forever from our lives.

All this was far in the future! That night, I could not have foreseen any of it. Nor how, over thirty years later, on the eve of Valentine's Day, I would remove from its hiding place at the bottom of a bureau drawer a bloodstained man's handkerchief initialed *JNL*, fine white cotton yellowed with time, and sr its wrinkles with the edge of my hand, and lift it to my fa Veronica her veil.

* * *

By the time Mr. Lacey and I left the Bison Diner, the light there had become blinding and the jukebox music almost deafening. My head would echo for days, *Lonely? lonely? lonely?* Mr. Lacey drove us hurriedly south on Huron Street, passing close beneath factory smokestacks rimmed at their tops with bluish-orange flame, spewing clouds of gray smoke that, upon impact with the freezing wind off Lake Erie, coalesced into fine gritty particles and fell back to earth like hail. These particles drummed on the roof, windshield, and hood of the Volkswagen, bouncing and ricocheting off, denting the metal. *God damn*, Mr. Lacey swore softly, *will You never cease!*

Abruptly then we were home. At my aunt's shabby wood-frame bungalow at 3998 Huron Street, Buffalo, New York, that might have been anyone of dozens, hundreds, even thousands of similar woodframe one-and-a-half-story bungalows in working-class neighborhoods of the city. The moon had vanished as if it had never been and the sky was depthless as a black paper cut-out, but a streetlamp illuminated the mouth of the snowed-in alley and the great snowdrift in the shape of a right-angled triangle lifting to the roof below my window. *What did I promise, Erin?— no one knows you were ever gone.* Mr. Lacey's words seemed to reverberate in my head without his speaking aloud.

With relief I saw that the downstairs windows of the house were all darkened, but there was a faint flickering light up in my room—the candle still burning, after all these hours. Gripping my hand tightly, Mr. Lacey led me up the snowdrift as up a treacherous stairway, fitting his boots to the footprints he'd originally made, and I followed suit, desperate not to slip and fall. *Safe at home, safe at home!* Mr. Lacey's words sounded close in my ears, unless it was, *Safe alone, safe alone!* I heard. Oh! the window was frozen shut again! so the two of us tugged, tugged, tugged, Mr. Lacey with good-humored patience, until finally ice shattered and the window lurched up to a height of perhaps twelve inches.

' begun to cry, a sorry spectacle, and my eyelashes had frozen within seconds in the bitter cold so Mr. Lacey laughed kissing my left eye, and then my right eye, and the lashes were thawed, and I heard, *Goodbye, Erin!* as I climbed back through the window.

THE ODD

BY ED PARK

Central Business District

"Welcome back to the Strange," the boy says. "It's a full house here at the Bizarre."

His mother laughs. It's a little warmer now, and quiet.

"You do it," the boy says.

"The Weird is packed to the rafters and the fans are going wild."

"Why are they going wild?" he asks. "Tell me again."

He has made the request six times tonight, voice full of love and wonder, and it will be the sixth time she complies. There is no other story to tell. The story is why they're here. They need to sleep. But first she must enter words into the silence, because the silence is too great.

"Close your eyes," she says, "and I'll tell you what I remember."

"They're already closed."

"Good."

She has to pick her words carefully, at least to begin with. Otherwise the kid will have a fit.

"At center ice, wearing number 11, is Gilbert Perreault from Victoriaville, Quebec. Acquired the first year the Sabres were in business."

"On left wing."

"On left wing is Rick Martin, and on right wing is René Robert."

"Both acquired the second year."

"Correct."

"Together known as?"

"Together known as," she says, and then the two of them together: "The French Connection."

She does it a little differently this time, with a French accent: *Ze Fransh Connectione*.

The boy laughs. "And who are the Sabres playing tonight?"

"Tonight they are playing the Philadelphia Flyers in the third game of the 1975 Stanley Cup finals."

"Almost twenty-five years ago," he says.

"Almost twenty-five years ago."

"The only time the Sabres have been this close to the cup," he says. Everything he says is so serious it cracks her up. Usually she tries to hold it in but tonight they need to laugh.

"Yes."

"We won't even get into the 'no goal' business."

"We're steering clear."

"The fucking Dallas Stars."

She can't help it: she laughs. He has his father's mouth.

"Dallas isn't even a hockey town," he continues. "It's never snowed there. Not in a million years."

"Philly gets snow," she says.

"Have you ever been there?"

"Just once, when I was a girl. I saw the Liberty Bell."

"Can I see it someday?"

"Yes, honey." She squeezes his hand. "Of course you can."

He squeezes back and takes his hand away. "Back to the game."

"Back to the game. The Sabres are in the finals. They trounced the Black Hawks and defeated the Canadiens and here they are."

"The Chicago Black Hawks in the *quarterfinals* and the Montreal Canadiens in the *semis*."

"Yes."

"Say it right." He is, she thinks, a bit Strange. Sometimes

he's even Bizarre. But then so is everyone. Peculiar. Unusual. Out of the Ordinary. Her thing is that she always liked the dare part of truth or dare. She would pick it every time.

"The Black Hawks in the quarterfinals and the Canadiens in the semis," she says. "They're two games into the finals against the Philadelphia Flyers."

"Good. Is this the first home game?"

"This is the first home game in the series for the Sabres. They are down two games in the series."

"The crowd is roaring at the Totally Weird."

"Yes, the crowd is roaring. Perreault is at center, wearing number 11. Rick Martin at left wing, number 7. Rene Robert is number 14."

"Spell René."

"R-E-N-É."

"There was a girl named Renee in my class."

"Different spelling. For a girl, there's one extra *e*." He brought her up earlier in the day, when she was telling the story. She can't quite picture the girl.

"Spell his last name."

"R-O-B-E-R-T."

"How come you say it *row-bear*?"

"That's how a French person would say it."

"They are all from Canada and they all speak French. Their English isn't very good."

"Well, they could speak English, but they definitely had thick French accents."

"And so they were called the French Connection."

"Yes."

"What were they connecting?"

She breathes for a while. She has a cigarette but she's good about not smoking in front of the kid. She wonders how long that policy will hold.

"Think of them passing the puck," she says at last. "The

puck is like a line that connects one stick to the other. On and on down the ice, passing, passing."

"Then shooting."

"Exactly."

"Right into the goal."

"Bingo."

"In front of a capacity crowd at the Strange, the Bizarre, the Totally Weird."

"Yes, baby." She clutches his hand.

"Don't call me *baby*. I'm not a baby."

"I can't help it. You're still my baby."

He lets it slide. He holds her hand tighter.

"There was a movie called *The French Connection* that came out around the same time. I never saw it."

"Can we rent it someday?"

"Someday. It's not really for kids." It must be milder than the video games he's been glued to since age four.

"What's it about?"

"I don't know that I've ever seen it. There are policemen and bad guys."

"Robbers?"

"Maybe."

"Murderers?"

"They probably kill some people. I'm not sure. Does it take place in France? Maybe. There's a famous actor named Gene Hackman who's in it."

"Is he dead?"

"No. I don't know. I don't think so."

Somewhere a drop of water lands in bigger water.

"Are we going to die?"

"We're not going to die." She kisses his head. "We're not."

"Tell me about the fog."

"Okay. On the night of the game, it's very warm in Buffalo, and the rink doesn't have air-conditioning."

He hoots like that's the most absurd thing imaginable. "No air-conditioning!"

As if on cue, a ghostly wind rolls over them. She can hear its progress beyond, rattling equipment, making a loose panel creak.

"Well, it's May, and May usually isn't so hot in Buffalo. It's a strange night. Even before the puck drops, a layer of fog covers the ice. And as the game goes on, the fog thickens until the players have trouble seeing. I remember there were workers who had to skate between periods with giant sheets and banners to try to clear the fog. But it just seemed to get harder and harder to see."

"You were in the crowd that night. That night at the Curious."

"I was in the crowd that night," she says. "In the Curious."

"The Bizarre. The Unusual."

"Yes. The Totally Weird. With your grandfather and your great-uncle and my cousins."

"How old were you?"

He knows the answer. "I turned seven that night."

"It was your birthday!"

"It was. Still is. May 20."

"May 20. One week after mine." He loves that they are both the same zodiac sign, Taurus. "But how did you get tickets?"

Again, he knows the answer. This part she has to get right. The silence swells until she thinks she's hearing things again. A trickle of water, a pipe crashing through plaster. "These were the hottest tickets in town, as you can imagine," she says, then waits because she knows he will repeat.

"The hottest tickets in town," he says.

"The night before the game, my cousin Jenny was listening to the radio, and they were giving away tickets to the fifty-fifth caller."

"Why fifty-fifth?"

"The station was WGR 550, and everyone called it GR 55. Jenny was supposed to be concentrating on her homework but she had the radio on, softly."

This is the boy's favorite part. "Then what happens?"

"In those days, kids didn't have their own phones. There were no cell phones at all. Most houses had only one or two phones, one in the kitchen, maybe another one upstairs. When she heard that the station was giving away tickets, she had to figure out how to get to the phone in her parents' bedroom. They were downstairs, so she thought the coast was clear. She made it into the bedroom and picked up the receiver."

"Then what happens?"

She thinks about her cell phone, traces its outline in her handbag. How long ago did it die? Did her text even go through? She has lost all sense of time. Maybe morning is on the way. The edges of the room seem to be paler. It might be her eyes seeing what isn't there, the way her ears hear things that aren't there.

"Jenny dialed one number, two numbers, three numbers," she continues, back on script. "Then she heard someone coming upstairs. It was her dad! He was calling her name."

"What did she do? Mom, what did she do?"

"Jenny dialed the last four numbers and held her breath. The bedroom was totally dark. Through the crack of the door she could see her father's shadow pass as he went to look in her room."

"He was saying, *Jenny, Jenny, how's the homework coming along?*"

"Right. He was pretty strict about schoolwork. He wanted her to do well in school and learn a lot."

"School is important?"

She chokes up. Her boy has had some trouble this year. He might have to repeat the grade. "It's important, but a lot of things are important."

"Then what happens?"

"Jenny dials the last three numbers." It occurs to her to add a detail absent from the previous tellings. "All the houses back then had what they called a rotary phone. The phones didn't have push-buttons back then. Think of a circle, a plastic circle, with holes as big as your fingertip all along the edge. You pick the number you want, pull it as far down as it can go, and then let it zip back into position. Then you do the next number."

"I don't get it."

She explains some more, traces a big circle and smaller circles on the back of his hand. But it's impossible to show how rotary phones work, here in the dark. As futile as describing how dinosaurs moved or how the pyramids were built, or the way your eyeballs flip an image upside down to your brain.

She senses his confusion. The confusion that gets him mad. This has been a problem lately at school. At home. Everywhere. He's been hitting other kids. He's been hitting her.

She thinks of something. "Guess what? I've been telling the story wrong."

"You have?"

"I always think of the game being foggy from the very start. But it wasn't. It didn't get foggy until the bat."

"Tell about the bat."

He loves the bat. "When I think of it now, the place is like a haunted house. It's the first home game for the Sabres. We're the host. And even before the game begins, people start seeing something flapping, falling. At first it looks like a piece of trash, some pages from a magazine. But then it never hits the ground. It keeps going up and zooming down and going up again."

"A bat. A bat in the Weird. A bat in the Eccentric."

"That's right. A bat in the Peculiar." *A bat in the Batshit*, she nearly says.

"What happened with Lorentz?"

"Play gets underway. You can't imagine the noise. People are shouting the whole time. Jim Lorentz sees the bat and lifts his stick and hits it."

"And it's dead."

"It's dead."

"What number was he?"

"Lorentz? I can't remember. I just remember Gil Perreault and Rick Martin and René Robert, 7, 11, 14."

"Then what happens?"

"They get the bat off the ice. And *then* the fog starts. That's the part I messed up. There was no fog till the bat."

"Till the bat was killed."

"Yes," she says. "Till the bat was killed."

A noise high above. Faint, but they both hear it. He moves closer to her. They heard voices before, two or ten hours ago, or they both imagined it at the same time—men moving through the building. They should have called out, then. Before the boy dropped the flashlight and it rolled between two old vending machines, impossible to move. Before her cell phone died. Before a weak panel gave way and dumped them, gently, to this dark room where they wait for the morning.

The noise came again, still soft but closer. "Was that a bat?"

"No, honey."

"Bats, bats, bats," he cries. "There are bats in the Odd!"

His voice echoes in the bowels of the huge wreck they're in, abandoned for a decade and marked off with tape. Tape in tatters, tape you could slip under with a kid for a quick look. Quick tour, show him your roots. She always liked a dare. A fence with a hole, she'd go through, didn't matter what was on the other side. They were just passing through town and here was this monument, unprotected. A firsthand history lesson for the boy who has some behavior issues, who is Peculiar, Unusual, occasionally a bit Bizarre. Show him the shell of Memorial Auditorium, what everyone used to call the Aud.

GOOD NEIGHBORS

BY GARY EARL ROSS

Allentown

By the time the Washingtons moved into the house two
doors away late last summer, Loukas and Athena Demopoulos had lived next to Helen Schildkraut for nearly
five years. Nestled in the heart of Allentown—a neighborhood
known for its Victorian-style homes and antique shops—theirs
was a short street with modest older houses, narrow driveways
that led to peeling garages, and countless trees—elm, oak, ma-
ple. The trees formed a lush green canopy in summer and left
everyone's lawn awash in brown, gold, and red leaves in the fall.
In fact, it was autumn leaves that alerted Lou to the competition.

Lou and Athena had moved into the smaller clapboard
house years after their three sons left their sprawling North Buffalo home—the first for college, the second for the army, and
the third for the state penitentiary. They had sold their thriv-
ing Greek restaurant for a sum that would support a modest
lifestyle. Still too young to collect Social Security, they retired
to Allentown instead of Florida because Athena insisted on remaining a bus ride away from Niko, her favorite, until he completed his sentence or made parole. A short, bony woman with
busy fingers, arched eyebrows, and perpetually pursed lips, she
wore dark clothing, even in summer. Her favorite pastime was
straightening out her two ungrateful daughters-in-law, who kept
her other sons chained to faraway Dallas, Texas, and Fort Benning, Georgia, but she looked forward to growing tomatoes and
squash in their postage stamp of a backyard. Lou looked forward
to wandering through nearby antique stores and criticizing the

lamb souvlaki and spanakopita at the Towne Restaurant. That he would even set foot in the Towne—for many years a rival of Demeter's, his place on Hertel—was to Lou an act of great generosity, an acknowledgment that the competition was finally over. Besides, the new owners had made such a mess of Demeter's that it hurt to go back, and the Towne was walking distance from his new home, its corner location close to several antique shops on Allen and Elmwood.

Lou liked old things, an interest he had developed after selling for a pittance the complete Depression glass dish set Georgie's wife Mary had left in his attic for safekeeping while they looked for a home in Dallas. Less than chastened by the girl's rage, he had suggested that his son learn to control his wife. Still, he had listened and understood his mistake, resolving never to repeat it. If he could be said to have a hobby, then, it would be antiquing. But the word *hobby* wasn't entirely accurate. Though he used the computer Spiro gave him to study the value of silver tea sets, gilt-edged china, Hummel figurines, ivory-handled utensils, vintage sewing machines and typewriters, gold pocket watches with chains intact, gramophones and music cylinders, porcelain dolls, paper dolls, wooden and metal toy trucks, tin product signs, stamped cookie tins, Avon bottles, well-kept furniture, and other detritus of bygone eras—he didn't build collections, as true hobbyists did. He searched dark, dusty shops for items he could sell quickly for the biggest possible profit. He liked old things if and only if he could flip them.

Helen Schildkraut was an old thing. She had papery skin, brittle white hair, abundant liver spots on her hands, and tired, rheumy eyes that might once have been green. Lou met Helen over the fence one day and later told Athena, "That old girl's gotta be pushin' eighty if not pullin' it." He liked the line so much he kept repeating it—in less-than-clever contexts. Pushing three hundred if not pulling it certainly applied to his fat cousin Markos, but pushing diarrhea if not pulling it when the Towne didn't

166 // BUFFALO NOIR

seat him quickly enough made no sense, and pushing ugly if not pulling it for Spiro's wife at Fort Benning was just plain mean. In their nearly forty years together Athena never laughed at his jokes, or, for that matter, at anyone else's, but the insult to her daughter-in-law did bring a small smile to her lips. She was at first indifferent to Helen and told Lou, "You like old stuff so much, you be her friend." He forgot his wife's comment until Helen saw him out front one day and asked if he could help open a stuck cabinet door.

Mounting the porch steps and entering through the front door, he had to walk through the parlor and the dining room to get to her kitchen. Wiry and robust, Lou was used to walking fast but found himself moving in slow motion. Though he had seen the leaded glass windows from outside, he had given little thought to what lay behind the curtains. Now every corner was a revelation, furnished with antiques, from knickknacks in mirror shadow boxes to elaborate table lamps with crystal teardrops dangling from their shades to marble-topped end tables to a clock in the belly of a leaping brass lion to pieces of furniture that predated FDR. She had a crystal chandelier, a grandfather clock with gold-flaked numerals, and a claw-foot mahogany china cabinet full of gilt-edged, gold-leaf, Depression-green, and milky-blue treasures, from teacups and bowls to platters, butter dishes, and candlesticks. After he jerked open the stuck cabinet door and sanded the edges, he stayed for afternoon tea.

"You won't believe the stuff she's got," he said to Athena at dinner that evening. Face flushed enough to ignite the roots of the few gray hairs left near his forehead, he described the pieces he'd seen, estimating their value because he had not yet gone online to check. When he finished, he sat back with a self-satisfied grin that made his wife narrow her eyes at him and purse her lips even more.

"Don't matter what she got, Lou," Athena replied. "Ain't your stuff."

"We talked this afternoon," Lou said, pausing to let his sentence sink in. "We talked a lot, Helen and me. She's a widow."

Athena sucked her teeth. "So now she Helen, not old girl or Miss Whats-her-kraut."

Lou dismissed her with a wave of his hand. "One daughter, who died unmarried. Two sisters, both dead without children. Her husband was an only child. No nieces or nephews from either side of the family. No cousins. No bridge club. No garden club. No friends who come to visit. Don't go to church or give to charity. Used to have a hairdresser who made house calls but he died. Used to have a handyman but he died too."

Athena snorted. "Lonely old woman." She shook her head hard. "God forbid that's what I be. Hope I go first."

"You're missing the point," Lou said. "She's got nobody in the world and needs stuff done. She's tired of depending on neighborhood kids to cut the grass and shovel the snow."

"So?"

"So she's eighty-six, with a house full of stuff worth a small fortune and nobody to leave it to."

"Very small but enough for you, eh? So to get into will you gonna be her handyman and new best friend—for dusty dishes and dirty lamps and some tiger with a clock in his ass." She shook her head in unmasked disgust.

"In the belly," Lou said, "and it's a lion."

Athena snorted again. "Whatever. Ain't worth time you'll put in." She shrugged. "But is your time to waste. Just don't rub your hands together till you find something worth real money. Then you get back to me."

He got back to Athena a week later, after Helen activated the automatic garage door opener to give him access to the rakes and lawn tools and he first saw the old car covered with a large canvas tarp. Checking to make sure Helen wasn't looking at him through the kitchen window, he lifted the back end of the canvas and felt his throat close. Heart pounding and mind racing, he raked and bagged leaves as quickly as he could that afternoon. The moment he got home he hit the Internet and let out a long breath when he found what he was seeking.

That evening at dinner he smiled as he told his wife about the car, a navy-blue, front-wheel-drive 1936 Cord 810 convertible—in mint condition, if he could judge from the rear end. Even with four flat tires, it was worth at least eighty or ninety grand, maybe even as much as a quarter million.

Athena didn't offer a single snort and let Lou introduce her to Helen the next day.

Athena joined Helen for tea one afternoon each week, sometimes taking her baklava or tiropita or some other flaky delight wrapped in phyllo dough. Sometimes she took Helen shopping for groceries, which consisted mainly of Salisbury steak and fried chicken TV dinners. Sometimes they went for ice cream, which Helen loved. Meanwhile, Lou took care of Helen's yard work and rolled out her trash tote the night before garbage collection day. He replaced her crusty rotary dial telephone with a sleek desk model that featured large buttons and caller ID. The evening her power went out and she called in a panic, he took her some of his famous chicken souvlaki, which she ate by candlelight as he went into the dank basement with his flashlight and searched for the fuse box. As the days shortened and temperatures fell, Lou returned to the basement and came up with her cobwebbed storm windows, which he cleaned and hung. He also brought over his caulking gun to seal off her house from drafts. By the beginning of November, Helen had dined with them four times. On the third occasion she wept as she told them how grateful she was for this newfound friendship. On the fourth, having tried her hand at cooking for the first time in decades, she contributed some God-awful German thing that left both Lou and Athena with such indigestion they couldn't sleep.

That year they went to Dallas for Christmas, and Athena

complained so much about the mattress that Georgie and Mary surrendered their own bed after the first night and slept in the guest room themselves. While Lou went golfing with Georgie the next day, Athena spent twenty minutes with Christina and Ari—in kindergarten and third grade, respectively—then followed Mary about the house, finding fault with the decor and the furniture and the window treatments, as well as with Mary's parenting and housekeeping skills. That evening, when Lou telephoned Helen to let her know they had arrived safely and would return in a week, neither he nor Athena noticed the looks of contempt Mary shot Georgie or the tension in their clenched jaws. Two afternoons later, having finally mastered the caller ID, Helen rang back and in a quavering voice told them how much she missed them and wished they would come home. The instant she hung up, they booked seats on a flight out the next day, Christmas Eve. In the morning neither Lou nor Athena noticed Mary's smile as Georgie loaded their luggage into the minivan and backed into the street to take his parents to the airport.

It wasn't until late January at one of their now weekly Thursday dinners that Helen mentioned her will. In a blue dress and pearls, she looked small in her chair—*her* chair, Lou reflected, because neither he nor Athena ever sat in it anymore, even when Helen wasn't there. She gazed at Lou, seated on her right, and then Athena, on her left, and said their many kindnesses would not go unrewarded.

"I don't have much," she said. "Just an old house with old things nobody wants, and my husband's old car nobody's driven in sixty-odd years." As always when mentioning Heinrich, she dabbed her eyes. "He was much older than I, you know." They knew. "He'd be more than a hundred and ten now." They knew that too. "I was his legal secretary, but after a week we both just knew we were each other's destiny." She looked off for a moment, gazing into a distant corner. "Less than ten years together, but he was the love of my life. When he died I just couldn't bear to give away his things or sell the house he loved." She turned to Lou. "My sisters came to live with me. They were lovely girls, and we were happy together for many years. But now they're gone too." Her voice cracked, and she shifted her attention to Athena. "Until you two moved in, I had no one. I know an old house with old stuff isn't worth much to young people nowadays, but you leave the things you love to the people you love, and I love you both. I've put you in my will."

Of course, they protested, assuring her that hers was pleasant company and such a gesture wasn't necessary. But in bed that night Athena initiated sex, despite their having already done it that month. Afterward, on her back in the dark and tugging down her gown, she said, "Wonder how long she gonna live." She felt Lou shrug beside her.

"She's eighty-six and fragile as a robin's egg," he replied, pulling his boxers back up. "She can't live forever." Soon they drifted off to sleep, peaceful in the certainty that before long their fortune would improve substantially.

But live Helen did, all through that cold dark winter and into the sunny days of spring—as Lou and Athena ran her errands, shoveled her snow, cleaned her house, cleaned and set out her porch furniture, washed her clothes and her front windows, helped her plant flowers in her garden while Athena's garden languished, reset the cable box that sat atop her twenty-five-inch RCA color console every time she pushed the wrong buttons on the remote, gave her a microwave oven to make heating her TV dinners easier and then reset it every time she pushed the wrong buttons on the keypad, readjusted her electronic thermostat every time she disengaged the furnace by pushing the wrong buttons on the display panel, sat with her in her living room to watch *Wheel of Fortune* and *Jeopardy!* and reruns of *Gunsmoke* and *I Love Lucy*, sat at her bedside to hold her hand when she wasn't feeling well, and took her to this or that of her numerous doctors. The more time they spent with her, the more strength they discovered beneath her seemingly fragile exterior. They knew she suffered from shingles, psoriasis, alopecia, muscle tremors, osteoporosis, and memory loss, but were surprised to learn she had already survived two heart attacks, a quadruple bypass, stomach cancer, skin cancer, and back surgery.

Through the winter Lou had entertained half-serious thoughts of putting a pillow over Helen's face or snuffing the pilot light on her stove's back burners one night so the house would fill with natural gas. But episode after episode of one *CSI* show or another (along with a dream in which he shared a cell with his son Niko) convinced him he didn't know enough to hide the evidence of suffocation and wasn't yet desperate enough to take the chance. And the possibility of a gas explosion that would destroy his inheritance was all he needed to reject the stove idea. He had no choice but to face the truth. Helen Schildkraut was too stubborn to die. Stubborn himself, he couldn't help but admire her determination to live forever against the odds, and it was there that he found the strength to continue. After all, as he explained to Athena one evening, she didn't need them *every* day, just a few times a week for a total of ten or fifteen hours. The house, the antiques, the car—everything together might bring in $400,000. What were ten or fifteen hours a week in the face of such a payoff? And so, with their eyes on the prize, they settled into a routine that was at times difficult but manageable.

Despite a reported increase in the area's burglary rate, the Washingtons moved into the house on the other side of Helen's when she was ninety and Lou and Athena finally qualified for Social Security. Pete Washington was a tall, well-built, coffee-colored man with a bald head and a black mustache above an easy smile. His wife was petite, short-haired, and very dark. Before anyone in the neighborhood made their acquaintance, word went round that they were drug dealers or speculators who would flip the house or ghetto lottery winners who chose Allentown gentrification over a suburban McMansion. When someone engaged Ebere Washington in conversation at a local market, the news that she was from Nigeria was the only remnant of the exchange to make it back to the street and was enough to convince some of the wagging tongues that they were part of Buffalo's growing refugee population. Apparently, no one noticed the Buffalo State College faculty sticker on Pete's Camry or the Buffalo General Hospital sticker and MD license plate on Ebere's Prius.

As he often told others, Lou had no problem with black people. He'd worked with them, served them meals, and a few times hired them. Sure, there were some assholes, but anybody who worked his way out of wherever he'd been born, as he himself had done, was okay by him—not necessarily to be his friend, but okay. Having come to America later than Lou and having spent much of her life isolated at home raising her boys, Athena was less magnanimous than her husband when it came to race. *Some* of them, she supposed, were all right, but on the whole she thought they were trouble and said so to Helen during one of their afternoon teas.

"Oh, but Dr. Washington is different," Helen said, with mild reproach in her voice. "And such a nice man."

Athena set down her teacup. "You meet?"

"Over the fence last week." Helen smiled with a twinkle of something Athena could not understand in her eyes. "He's a professor. Isn't that wonderful? Heinrich often said all colored people needed was a chance. And the Washingtons are proof of it. The wife is a real doctor." She leaned forward, lowering her voice as if about to mention the unmentionable. "Ob-gyn." Then she sat back and clasped her hands in her lap. "And they have a son too, away at college in Chicago." She nodded. "Very nice people."

In bed, as he sat up reading one of his antiques guides, Athena told Lou about the Washingtons. Shrugging at her obvious discomfort, he said, "Good for him, and I guess a lady doc's okay if she knows her place as a wife." They weren't the first people of color in the area, he reminded her—in fact, there were lots of them, all kinds of coloreds from all over the world. A few days later, after he met Pete Washington—who seemed vaguely familiar—and shook his hand, he said to Athena, "Told you, I got no trouble with blacks."

It took Lou almost a month to recognize the danger posed by the newcomers. It was midafternoon of a bright fall Friday, and in golf shirt and walking shorts he was on his way home from visiting the antique shops that dotted Allen between Elmwood and Main. He had stopped at the Towne for a bite of saganaki, just enough to keep him till dinner, and rounded the corner of his street with visions of sinking into his recliner. But he saw that a lot of leaves had fallen since his morning departure and guessed his recliner would have to wait until he had raked the front lawns. But three or four doors from the corner he stopped and squinted at what he thought he saw eight or ten doors up the street.

It looked like somebody was raking Helen Schildkraut's lawn.

Lou hustled up the street, recognizing Pete Washington as the interloping landscaper. Worse, Pete was using Helen's old green plastic rake—which meant he'd been inside the garage and might have seen the Cord. Would he know what it was? Of course he would, Lou thought, if he saw it. He was a professor, smart. The question was, was he the kind of guy nosy enough to lift the tarp?

"Hey, Pete," Lou said. "What you up to?"

"Just raking." In polo shirt, shorts, and sandals, Pete stopped working and wiped his forehead with tissue he pulled from his pocket.

"Yeah?"

"I was doing my lawn and my rake fell apart. Helen saw me

through the window and offered to let me use hers. I'm just re-paying the favor."

Lou nodded, waiting.

"What?" Pete said.

"Just tired after my walk," Lou said. "So you were saying Helen gave you her rake."

"Nah," Pete said. He resumed dragging the long plastic tines through leaves. "She just opened her garage from inside the house with her remote and let me get it myself."

Lou hesitated. "Surprised you're not at work."

"My department meeting was canceled and I came home early. Ebere's at the hospital till eight tonight, so I'll have the house to myself for a while." He stopped raking. "And I can make her dinner. Candles. Music. Wine. I like to surprise her. Keeps things . . . interesting."

"You know," Lou said slowly, "I usually do Helen's lawn. You want to get started on your big night, I can take over."

Pete dismissed him with a wave of his hand. "Take a break, Lou. I got it. Besides, you might want to make dinner for *your* wife. Helen said you once owned a Greek restaurant."

"Yeah, Demeter's."

"Nice food. Used to have lunch there with some of my colleagues."

"That's where I seen you before," Lou said. "Been there lately?"

Pete shook his head. "It's different now, not as good."

Lou half smiled. "So what're you gonna make your wife? If you want some ideas . . ."

"I'm good, but whatever I decide, I'll make a little extra and take it over to Helen so she won't have to eat one of those crappy TV dinners. She's been so nice to us."

Lou nodded and bit his lip and began to drift toward his own front porch.

"By the way," Pete called after him, "have you seen that *car*?"

And just like that, the game was on.

Several times that fall Lou stepped next door to tackle a chore on his Helen List only to find Pete Washington had already completed the task. Pete's class schedule was such that he had a free morning here and a free afternoon there when he could sweep her porches or patch her blacktop drive. He took her shopping every now and then. Sometimes he even got to the yard work before Lou. He wasn't as thorough, but Helen didn't seem to mind. He never washed her front windows and didn't spend as much time inside her house as Lou and Athena, though he was definitely charming his way into her heart. Twice, when Ebere worked extra late in the hospital, Lou watched him carry a box from Just Pizza straight onto Helen's porch and take a seat so they could share it. One night Helen was ill, as she later told Athena over the back fence, and Mrs. Washington came over to examine her, giving her medicine that made her feel so much better. When her power failed in October, Pete not only replaced the blown fuse but also arranged for an electrician friend to install a breaker box the following Saturday, at a considerable discount. Lou still managed to roll out her garbage tote before each collection day but only because the professor had classes that afternoon. Once he put the tote on the curb so early a passing police officer stopped her cruiser and threatened to fine him if he didn't keep it in the yard till six.

"Dr. Washington says with all the burglaries around here I should have an alarm put in," Helen said at their now semi-regular Thursday dinner the first week in November. "But I have nothing that would interest thieves or dope addicts. What do you think?"

Athena, who still did her laundry but had grown more distant from the old woman since the Washingtons' arrival, had no opinion. Lou was slow to respond, unnerved by the look in Helen's eye when she spoke of Pete—not exactly a schoolgirl crush but something else that made him wary. Finally, he said, "Those things got panic buttons—you know, for police or fire or medical. Good thing to have."

Later, Lou sat bolt upright in bed when he realized what it was he'd seen in Helen's eyes every time she spoke of the Washingtons. It was an almost maternal pride, as if they were her children and she was living through their accomplishments. Though the newcomers gave no indication they knew they were in a competition, he decided he must do something to safeguard his inheritance. And he must do it before winter, before the younger man outshoveled him and lavished Helen with Christmas cookies and his doctor wife cured her of something and got her to change her will. However much you loved other people, it was the ones you loved as your children who got your estate.

At last he was desperate.

Lou might not have resorted to murder if Helen hadn't declined his Thanksgiving invitation in order to spend the holiday with Pete and Ebere. "Their son will be home," she had told Lou over the phone while Pete lay on his back to tighten the new trap he'd installed beneath her kitchen sink, "and they'd like me to meet him." Lou still might not have resorted to murder if Athena hadn't screamed at him so much when he gave her the news. "I cook for old bitch, clean for old bitch, be nice to old bitch 'cause you say so! You! Now look! We get nothing! Might as well go eat with Spiro and Horse-Face!" And he might not have resorted to murder if there hadn't been so many recent break-ins. But it was the rash of burglaries that made him stare up at the guest room ceiling in Spiro's house in Fort Benning. For three nights over the Thanksgiving weekend, he worked out the details. Sunday, his final night, he slept better than his two-year-old granddaughter in the next room.

Pete Washington had a late class every Monday night and got home sometime after nine. The Monday after Thanksgiving was warm enough that the threatened light snow came down as misty rain by the time Pete wheeled his Camry into his driveway. Tired from the morning flight home but still determined to see his plan through, Lou was waiting for him and rushed outside to meet him before he could enter his house through the side door. Right hand in the pocket of his slicker and left hand pointing up Helen's driveway, Lou said, "Pete, it's Helen! Come quick!"

If he had any doubt that Pete Washington wanted Helen's things as much as he did, it disappeared when he saw how quickly the man moved. Within three steps Pete was ahead of Lou, moving toward the rear of the house and calling Helen's name. He never saw Lou slip on the latex gloves and pull on the shower cap. When they were deep enough in the driveway that they couldn't be seen from the street, Lou pulled the fisherman's knife from his slicker pocket and jammed it into his rival's right kidney.

Pete gasped and clutched his back and stumbled forward, muttering something that showed his confusion. Then Lou was on him, forcing him into the dark yard, even though he tried to plant his feet and turn around. Left arm across the back of Pete's neck and right hand moving like a piston, Lou drove the knife into him again and again. With each blow another page of the plan unfolded in Lou's mind. The slicker would keep blood from staining his clothes. The cheap oversized shoes from Big K, the slicker, the gloves, the shower cap, and the knife would all be in a bundle wedged behind the washtub in his basement until later. The police would have no reason, no probable cause, to search Lou's house. No one could say he had ever exchanged an angry word with Pete Washington, likely another victim of random violence. The body would stay in the dark yard till morning. Helen herself would see it from her kitchen window and call the police. She would tell them that Dr. Washington often checked on her when he came home, just like Mr. and Mrs. Demopoulos on the other side. And they all had warned her to be careful with the recent break-ins. Maybe poor Pete had confronted a would-be burglar and died trying to stop him. Wasn't she fortunate to have such good neighbors?

Pete's knees were buckling when Lou gave him a hard shove around the back corner of the house. He collapsed five feet past the rear door as Lou moved toward him to deliver the final blow. At that instant, however, Lou found himself caught in the brilliant crossfire of motion-sensor lights that lit up the backyard like combat flares. The lights were part of the home security system that Helen, at Pete's insistence, had allowed his electrician friend to install over the Thanksgiving weekend. Lou wheeled toward the kitchen window and saw the equally startled Helen looking out at him. Taking her hand away from her mouth, she reached toward something he couldn't see, but he knew what it was even before the piercing alarm deafened him, roused the neighborhood, and connected directly to the nearest police station.

The panic button.

Eight months later, in early summer, Helen Schildkraut had new neighbors on either side of her, a young couple with three children in the Demopoulos house and two young men who told her they were partners, whatever that meant, in the Washington house. After the mess Lou had made of the neighborhood—for no good reason she could discern—she was glad the new people were all so nice. They helped her in the yard and took her shopping. They brought her food and adjusted the cable settings and the microwave again and again without complaint. Moving amid the timeworn relics that filled her house and still missing Heinrich after all these years, she never heard the husband tell his wife or the first partner tell the second about the car in her garage. If she had, she would have laughed it off. After all, who'd give a fig about that old thing?

HAND

BY KIM CHINQUEE

Historic District

Passing a girl on the sidewalk, Kyle notices her hand, so small with its plain fingers, unlike the hand he found in the dumpster. At first it didn't seem real. At first he only poked at it.

He hears a dog bark and he looks down into his cart at the cans. The hand felt kind of spongelike. It smelled of wine. He found it under soggy papers and some empty beer cans; he picked it up. He figures it's his now.

Across the street, he sees some cops sitting in their cars talking to each other. Kyle feels electric. His cart sounds like a train. The air feels thick, its smell reminding him of bacon.

As his stomach growls, he remembers he skipped breakfast. He usually has grits, something he's been eating since he was a kid. He'd be in his grandfather's old white shack, where he used to go every morning before school, his grandfather saying, "You must always tell the truth. No matter how anybody treats you." Kyle thought about that at school each day, trying to sit upright in his desk and listen to the teacher. One day his grandpa slipped his shack key into Kyle's pocket and said, "It's time." And the next morning when Kyle went there, he unlocked the door to find his grandpa hanging from the ceiling. Kyle was only ten. He still has the key; it sits there in his pocket.

Cars are beeping. His cart isn't full. Still. This other thing is something.

Kyle knows the right thing to do. But cops can be rude and nasty. He was a cop for two months in the air force—the other cops used to sit around and tell dirty jokes and swear, and since Kyle didn't do that, they kept calling him a faggot.

At home, he wheels his cart up to the building where he lives. He grabs the hand and puts it in his backpack. "Hand," he says, "we're going to my place."

He runs up, unlocks his door, pets his old Chihuahua, and when he sees the fridge he opens the door and sets the hand on a shelf.

When he gets down to the cart again, he watches a couple pass: a girl with dark-lined eyes, a white-haired man in golf shorts.

He pushes the cart to Tops, and with his giant hands he puts his cans and bottles into the machine.

Later Kyle puts on his newest jeans to get his blood drawn. He dons a crisp white shirt he used to wear when working in collections. He's had plenty of jobs: scrubbing toilets, his short gig as a cop, then that year as a med tech. He picked berries but wasn't fast enough. At thirty-six he tried to get a bachelor's in history. He thinks of his own history: flashbacks of his father in the bathroom, the barn and straw, and his mother's ruby glasses. Once a week his therapist tells him to watch the dots on a screen as she asks him to relive things.

She says, "How do you feel?"

He doesn't know what to say. "I'm not sure I've ever felt much."

Today he's getting his blood drawn, which he does every year on his doctor's orders. Kyle parks the car his father used to drive before ending up in prison for killing a woman while drunk driving. Sometimes Kyle visits the prison, busing the hour to get there. His father wears orange and keeps his head shaved. Each time as Kyle leaves, his father says, "You *must* be guilty of *something*."

Kyle walks to the lab, thinking of the hand with its fuchsia polish. He says hi to a lady on the sidewalk. But mostly to her shaggy dog, its tail wagging incessantly.

At the lab, Kyle skims through the stack of magazines, only seeing ones with skinny, fair-skinned ladies on the covers. On the chair next the table, he sees a thin man wearing tinted glasses and an obese lady with curly auburn hair. Kyle notices an odor. On the TV in the corner, a sportscaster talks about the Sabres' recent win. A weather lady says it's cloudy. Then there's breaking news; a pregnant, suited woman interviews a man who holds a slim cigar. He says, "A woman washed up in the river. She's been missing. Her name is Ruby Smith and she appears to have no hand."

Kyle moves closer to the screen, seeing a shot of the dead woman: dark-haired with a barrette, her face a little chubby. She's wearing glasses and maroon lipstick. She's maybe about thirty. When he found the hand, he didn't picture whom it might belong to. It was manicured and purple; the wrist was wrapped in foil. He looked at the palm and fingers. They seemed so soft and tender, like he remembers his mother's being. She left when he was twelve, and he wonders where she is now. The hand was wet, like it wasn't dead yet. He pictures it, now maybe next to the peanut butter in his fridge, how he left it there in haste, thinking he'd tend to it later.

The sportscaster comes back on the screen and talks about the upcoming Bills game. Kyle sits. He feels like a kid again, his father telling him he's sinful.

Then when the phlebotomist calls out, "Kyle Krupp," he follows her. He sits in the chair and sees a sign that reads, *Biohazard*. He remembers being on her end of the needle, the routine of gloving, uncapping, sticking, watching the blood rush into the tubing.

He studies the lab order, his last name spelled with one *p* instead of two. He says, "My last name is spelled wrong."

She says, "I'll have to fix it," then slams her hand down on the printer. Her lipstick looks black, and her nails are long and polished.

182 // Buffalo Noir

He remembers patient-sensitivity sessions he used to have to attend. They were required by law.

He says to her, "Have you been to the training?"

She turns to him. "What?"

He says, "Patient sensitivity. Have you not been trained?" He smells an odor and sees the obese woman going down the hallway.

The phlebotomist says, "I'll be back." She gets up and leaves, so Kyle sits and waits. He remembers chairs like this, back when he was a med tech, sitting down and discussing things like breaking up with his one and only girlfriend. She was a med tech too until she said she was moving on, maybe to save lost dogs or plant marigolds, maybe to hang out with bikers.

He thinks of the woman in the news, the hand. He thinks about the dead girl.

Now he hears the phlebotomist from across the hall. "Girl," she says, "that fat lady smells like sausage!"

"Girl," says someone else, "you always get the stinky ones."

Then another woman appears in the hallway sprinting backward. She stops, looking at Kyle. "Hey!" she yells down the hall to the other workers. "You guys," she yells again, "we have a patient!"

Kyle hears somebody say, "He was a pain right when he got here."

The woman from the hall looks at him again and says, "I'm really sorry."

On the way home, Kyle notices the *Check Engine* light on the dashboard of his Toyota, and hopes it doesn't need anything expensive. He can get by with his savings and from what he makes on bottles. He likes to compare prices.

He stops at a red light, seeing a driver in the next car who looks like the phlebotomist. His windows are open. He wonders if he took his medication. He tries to see her hands on the wheel—they look a little plain. He glances at his own hands. Big and bony. Wrinkled.

He thinks about the hand belonging to the dead girl. He feels his stomach churn. He remembers finding the hand, so manicured and soft. It didn't seem real.

He recalls that girlfriend from long ago, how she went to get her nails done. He thinks of his mother's hands, the last time he saw them.

At the apartment, Kyle remembers the barrette he saw in the picture of the dead girl. Blue and gold, a butterfly, like one he saw holding back his mother's bangs the night she left. There's another shot he remembers of his mother looking happy, by the way she holds her head back, her teeth and lips aglow. At the beach, the wind sweeping.

He sits on his sofa, listening to his dog whine.

The woman was last seen at the Pancake House on Hertel. Kyle pictures a woman with big rings, high heels, and good clothes in a mansion.

He wants wine. He goes to the fridge, where he sees her right hand where he left it. He picks it up and smells it. It reminds him of merlot; the skin is rubbery. He touches the foil on the end, and he imagines a big tree. He remembers a branch from his grandfather's oak that smashed onto his father's windshield in the middle of a snowstorm. "It's okay," he says out loud. He decides to make some eggs. He turns on the stove and pours himself some wine. He picks up the hand; he cradles it and rocks.

He wakes to the smell of smoke. He sees firemen and police who have sticks and cuffs and handguns. He sees the hand on his lap, and the empty wineglass by the rocker. A black man stands in front of him and says, "Busted."

The man takes the hand. Kyle's dog looks up at him. He got a dog bite as a kid, something he hasn't thought of in a while, as if it's all a dream or maybe never happened. He remembers the dog's sharp teeth, its black eyes, then being in the hospital with a wrist full of stitches.

"You almost burned the place down," says another cop with a uniform too small for his gigantic muscles.

Kyle remembers the night before, turning on the burner to make eggs, swallowing the Xanax his doctor said to take when he feels anxious. He reaches in his pocket, running his thumb over the edges of his grandpa's key.

The hand, it felt so cold, the skin almost like his mother's. He wanted to do right. He says, "But it's my hand."

He rides away in the backseat of the cop car. His own hands are in cuffs. He looks up at the rearview and sees the cop's white eyes.

Kyle says, "I didn't kill her."

He thinks he hears a laugh.

"I'm innocent," he says. "I'm sure of it. I know."

ABOUT THE CONTRIBUTORS

Christina Milletti

DIMITRI ANASTASOPOULOS was born in Athens, Greece. He is the author of *A Larger Sense of Harvey* and *Farm for Mutes*. Anastasopoulos teaches contemporary literature and creative writing at the University at Buffalo.

Philippe Matsas

LAWRENCE BLOCK, an internationally best-selling novelist, was born at Buffalo Children's Hospital, lived a few years at 2155 Delaware Avenue, a few more at 673 Parkside, and spent the rest of his youth at 422 Starin Avenue. He attended PS 66 (now North Park Academy) and Bennett High, where he was Class Poet in 1955. Most of his writing is set in New York City, his home for most of his adult life, but his Ehrengraf stories take place in Buffalo.

Kim Chinquee

KIM CHINQUEE is the author of the collections *Oh Baby, Pretty,* and *Pistol.* Her work has appeared in hundreds of journals and anthologies including *NOON,* the *Nation, Conjunctions, StoryQuarterly, Ploughshares, Denver Quarterly, The Pushcart Prize, Huffington Post,* and others. She is an associate editor of *New World Writing,* and an associate professor of English at SUNY–Buffalo State.

Justine Kalb Costello

BROOKE COSTELLO was born and raised in North Buffalo. He attended St Joseph's Collegiate Institute for Young Men, and Oberlin College. Window breaking and prank calling were his calling cards as a youth. He is currently working on two novels, *Gravquake* (science fiction) and *Jumpy's Game,* a noir set in the blizzard of 1977 in Buffalo. He lives in New York City with his wife Justine and sons Redd and Greer.

Anouchka de Williencourt

TOM FONTANA was born and raised on the West Side. Italian-Polish, he attended Canisius High and SUCB, from which he received an honorary doctorate in letters. Immediately after college, he worked at Studio Arena Theatre. He has done a lot of writing for TV, including *St. Elsewhere, Homicide, Oz, Copper,* and Netflix's *Borgia.* Fontana is now writing his first (and last) novel for HarperCollins. He proudly calls both Buffalo and New York City home.

BRIGID HUGHES is the founding editor of the literary magazine *A Public Space*, and a contributing editor at Graywolf Press. She was born and raised in Buffalo.

kc kratt

CHRISTINA MILLETTI is an associate professor of English at the University at Buffalo where she curates the Exhibit X Fiction Series and helped to found the new MA in English/Innovative Writing Program. Her collection of short stories, *The Religious & Other Fictions*, was published by Carnegie Mellon University Press. She has just finished a novel called *Choke Box* and is now at work on a new collection of fictions called *Erratics*.

Charlie Grosk

JOYCE CAROL OATES is a recipient of the National Medal of Humanities and the National Book Award. She grew up in the countryside north of Buffalo, and attended school in the suburb of Williamsville. Buffalo has been transmogrified into "Union City" in her novel *What I Lived For* and "Port Oriskany" in many other novels and stories. Oates edited both *New Jersey Noir* and *Prison Noir* for Akashic Books.

Sylvia Plachy

ED PARK was born in Buffalo in 1970. He is the author of the novel *Personal Days* and has been a newspaper, magazine, and book editor. He lives in New York City, where he and his sons continue to root for the Sabres and Bills.

Robyn Rohde

CONNIE PORTER is from Lackawanna, New York. She is the author of the *Addy* series of historical children's novels from American Girl. Her first novel, *All-Bright Court*, was set in Lackawanna. Her novel *Imani All Mine*, set in Buffalo, was named an Honor Book by the Black Caucus of the American Library Association. She lives in Las Vegas, and is a lifelong Bills fan.

Sublime Photography

LISSA MARIE REDMOND was born and raised in Western New York. She has been with the Buffalo Police Department since 1993. After making detective in 1999, she was assigned to the sex offense squad and later to the cold case homicide unit where she still works. Detective Redmond has a bachelor's degree from the State University at Buffalo. She lives and writes in South Buffalo with her police detective husband, Dan Redmond, and their two daughters.

kc kratt

GARY EARL ROSS, a novelist and playwright, is a retired University of Buffalo professor. His work includes the books *The Wheel of Desire, Shimmerville,* and *Blackbird Rising,* and the plays *Sleepwalker, Picture Perfect, The Best Woman, Murder Squared, The Scavenger's Daughter, Matter of Intent* (winner of the Edgar Award), *The Mark of Cain,* and *The Guns of Christmas.* He is at work on the Buffalo-based Gideon Rimes mystery series. For more information visit www.garyearlross.net.

Ashley Gilbertson

S.J. ROZAN is the author of fifteen novels and four dozen short stories and has edited two anthologies, one of which is *Bronx Noir* from Akashic Books. Though she was born in the Bronx, family lore always maintained she was conceived in Buffalo. Like a bad penny, she returned there for graduate school, living for four years near the old University of Buffalo campus. For more information visit www.sjrozan.net.

Cheryl Huber

JOHN WRAY is the author of the novels *The Right Hand of Sleep, Canaan's Tongue,* and *Lowboy.* His fourth novel, *The Lost Times Accidents,* is forthcoming from Farrar, Straus & Giroux.

Also available from the Akashic Noir Series

BROOKLYN NOIR
edited by Tim McLoughlin
320 pages, trade paperback original, $15.95

THE INAUGURAL TITLE in the Akashic Noir Series, *Brooklyn Noir* features Edgar Award finalist "The Book Signing" by Pete Hamill, MWA Robert L. Fish Memorial Award winner "Can't Catch Me" by Thomas Morrissey, and Shamus Award winner "Hasidic Noir" by Pearl Abraham.

BRAND-NEW STORIES BY: Pete Hamill, Nelson George, Sidney Offit, Arthur Nersesian, Pearl Abraham, Neal Pollack, Ken Bruen, Ellen Miller, Maggie Estep, Kenji Jasper, Adam Mansbach, Nicole Blackman, C.J. Sullivan, Chris Niles, Norman Kelley, Tim McLoughlin, Thomas Morrissey, Lou Manfredo, Luciano Guerriero, and Robert Knightly.

MANHATTAN NOIR
edited by Lawrence Block
264 pages, trade paperback original, $15.95

BRAND-NEW STORIES BY: Jeffery Deaver, Lawrence Block, Charles Ardai, Carol Lea Benjamin, Thomas H. Cook, Jim Fusilli, Robert Knightly, John Lutz, Liz Martínez, Maan Meyers, Martin Meyers, S.J. Rozan, Justin Scott, C.J. Sullivan, and Xu Xi.

"A pleasing variety of Manhattan neighborhoods come to life in Block's solid anthology . . . the writing is of a high order and a nice mix of styles." —*Publishers Weekly*

"A fun read that's sure to please mystery lovers and fans of New York fiction." —*About.com*

QUEENS NOIR
edited by Robert Knightly
352 pages, trade paperback original, $15.95

BRAND-NEW STORIES BY: Denis Hamill, Maggie Estep, Megan Abbott, Robert Knightly, Liz Martínez, Jill Eisenstadt, Mary Byrne, Tori Carrington, Shailly P. Agnihotri, K.j.a. Wishnia, Victoria Eng, Alan Gordon, Belinda Farley, Joseph Guglielmelli, Patricia King, Kim Sykes, Jillian Abbott, Stephen Solomita, and Glenville Lovell.

"Queens has a dark side, a very dark side . . . a particularly fertile ground for the eerily ironic . . . 352 pages of wickedness." —*New York Daily News*

"Just when you thought you couldn't get any more attitude in Queens, along came *Queens Noir* to make the mean streets meaner." —*TimesLedger*

•

BRONX NOIR
edited by S.J. Rozan
368 pages, trade paperback original, $15.95

BRAND-NEW STORIES BY: Jerome Charyn, Terrence Cheng, Joanne Dobson, Rita Lakin, Lawrence Block, Suzanne Chazin, Kevin Baker, Abraham Rodriguez, Jr., Steven Torres, S.J. Rozan, Thomas Bentil, Marlon James, Sandra Kitt, Robert J. Hughes, Miles Marshall Lewis, Joseph Wallace, Ed Dee, Patrick W. Picciarelli, and Thomas Adcock

"Dark tales of murder and mayhem . . . conniving plots by grifters, drifters and sociopaths . . . the characters' failures are the book's success." —*New York Daily News*

STATEN ISLAND NOIR
edited by Patricia Smith
256 pages, trade paperback original, $15.95

Featuring the Robert L. Fish Memorial Award–winning story "When They Are Done with Us" by Patricia Smith

BRAND-NEW STORIES BY: Bill Loehfelm, S.J. Rozan, Ted Anthony, Todd Craig, Ashley Dawson, Bruce DeSilva, Louisa Ermelino, Binnie Kirshenbaum, Michael Largo, Michael Penncavage, Linda Nieves-Powell, Eddie Joyce, Shay Youngblood, and Patricia Smith.

"Staten Island, the last of New York City's five boroughs to enter Akashic's noir series, serves as the setting for this exceptionally strong anthology." —*Publishers Weekly* (starred review)

TORONTO NOIR
edited by Janine Armin & Nathaniel G. Moore
288 pages, trade paperback original, $15.95

BRAND-NEW STORIES BY: RM Vaughan, Nathan Sellyn, Ibi Kaslik, Peter Robinson, Heather Birrell, Sean Dixon, Raywat Deonandan, Christine Murray, Gail Bowen, Emily Schultz, Andrew Pyper, Kim Moritsugu, Mark Sinnett, George Elliott Clarke, Pasha Malla, and Michael Redhill.

"Armin and Moore assemble a collection of Toronto tales that will delight readers anywhere . . . Whether you love Toronto or hate it, this smart, stylish collection will suit you. Those who love the city can wallow in the fine writing about local icons; haters can feast on the city's Toronto-centricism." —*Globe and Mail*